PETER TRUE

THE EARLY YEARS

DANIECE
FOR THE INNER BOY
MAY HE NEVER
LEAVE YOU

PRELUDE

I'm really under 7 at heart.

Maybe we all are. We don't want this constant pressure to strive, to achieve. Even those lucky enough to win, win, win, always seem to lose something. Like their wives. Or husbands. Partners. Some (or a lot) of their money. Respect. Love.

We just want to stay young. Very young. Just pure.

And some of us, once we're back there, want to show the world what they've been missing.

Like playing the pianola.

Because if you haven't ever pedaled on a pianola, you haven't lived. Really. More importantly, if you didn't pedal on a pianola before the age of 5, you never understood the true essence of sensitivity. Which is? One small boy in harmony with ivory and strings.

They'd come, the adults, in their droves, come to the Phantas-magorically Phenomenal Pianola and its Extremely Excellent Exponent. And the Little Lad. He'd give them a comprehensive tour of his handsome artefact, replete with potted history and "the best way to play it". Then offer them the opportunity to do their bit. And pedal furiously. And lo, all they'd get would be a weak little groaning from the piano's innards. A few tinkly moments. That would be that. And then the little boy-prodigy-maestro would puff his chest out. Sit down with pride on the oversized piano stool. Gather himself. Set the tempo lever - 60 for slow, 70 for mid tempo, 80 for fast - allegro of course. And off we'd go.

There were words, of course

Troubles really are bubbles they say
And I'm bubbling over today
Spring brings roses to people you see
But it brings hay fever to me
If I ever had luck
It's bad luck for sure
And Pollyanna stuff too
Is tough to endure

Where's that rainbow they hear about?
Where's that lining they cheer about?
Where's that love nest,
where love is king ever after?

Where's that blue room they sing about?
Where's that sunshine they fling about?
I know morning will come,
but pardon my laughter!

In each scenario
you can depend on the end
where the lovers agree.
Where's that Lothario?
Where does he roam, with his dome
vaselined as can be?

It is easy to see all right
Everything's gonna be all right
Be just dandy for everybody but me.
There we'd all be, in the music bubble. Rodgers, Kern, Gershwin, that geezer who wrote "Halfway up the Stairs".

And me.

CHAPTER 1

1 boy, 25 girls

Little boys and girls really are small. I mean the ones between about four and seven. So small you probably wouldn't notice them.

If you bothered and if you talked to them a bit - or rather, let them talk to you - you might think they were surprisingly funny. Or rude. Or extremely intelligent for their age.

You'd be very surprised.

But why? They're just a miniature version of you, of all of us. Most of what they're at or where they're going, is in the DNA. So say the experts.

It might not be believable for most of the time. After all, they need care and love more than those more senior of us. That's mostly because they're physically smaller and weaker and of course because they don't have that most golden of things - experience.

And all of this is all too easy to forget, isn't it? Mostly the modern excuse is that we're too busy. That's rubbish of course. We just can't be bothered, that's the real reason.

We forget ourselves all too often. Forget who we are, where we come from, how we feel, how we felt, how we were young once. There's always far too much to worry about now to worry about then. In any case, there's nothing to gain, to learn from. Nostalgia's just trash, isn't it?

When we come to look at those cutesy little brats we've already forgotten ourselves. Most of us can't remember what time of day it is, let alone what it felt to be very young.

Well I can tell you this. Kids of four are nobody's fools. They know whether you've made a mistake by buying that dress you think goes rather well with your eyes. They know it hugs you a little too tightly. Or that car Dad bought. What was he thinking? And they understand that their siblings are conniving, thieving, selfish tosspots who should go find a lake and jump in it.

They're four. They know the score.

And I, for one, was four and pretty much in charge. I could carry on a conversation with uncles, cousins and aunts as well as anyone. In any case, they all talked to me because they loved me. They loved me because I was so well behaved, a nice boy. So nice in fact that, when I was 6 months old, they'd say I was so quiet and serene that something must be wrong with me. So Mum used to say. Frequently.

I smiled a lot. Just about every day there'd be someone for me to smile at. At nursery school I had my girlie friends and my boysie friends. They liked me. I smiled at them - well, most of them. There was a girl called Mary who was peevish to everyone but she doesn't really count. I still smiled at her. Actually, I was in love with her. But that's another story. No, apart from her, everyone liked me. And loved me. Jasper loved me. Buffy loved me. Ian loved me. Becky loved me. I smiled at them. I loved them back.

My parents loved me. Even my sisters loved me, to an acceptable extent, I thought.

I'd experienced all the lovely things you can do up until 4. I'd been on holiday, many times. Fabulous places - Crackington Haven, Lyme Regis, The Lake District, Portmeirion. I lived in a big house, all on its own. I'd been given my own record player, with a whole case of colourful 45s. I had a toy dog that did cartwheels and had my own milk truck. I might have chewed the bottles to nothingness but I still had that truck.

And I could play the pianola better than anyone, anywhere.

It was all set up. Ready for the next stage of my life. They called it "school". It'd be easy.

Oh it was. It really was. And it was the best place.

But it was the worst place, too. It wasn't the school. The school was perfect.

It was the decision to send me there in the first place.

Because at four years, 10 months and 20 days, Peter, the completely happy and in control little boy, was sent to a girl's school.

You don't know it's all about to change at the time, of course you don't. One day you're learning to tie your shoelaces, the next a tie. The day after that you've tried it all on. The crisp nylon shirt, blue and green tie, green v-necked jumper with the green and blue neckband. The shorts. The cap. There you go, the perfect little schoolboy. Except....

No, you don't know it's all about to change, that it's a little strange. In fact the first time I was there it was all very normal actually. For some reason I remember it clearly though I'm really not sure why. It wasn't a particularly eventful day. It was the Open Day, possibly a couple of weeks before the school opened for Autumn Term. I was just sitting there. In the sandpit. With Mum gassing to a stranger.

You'd have loved Mum. Everybody did, eventually. But one thing I never quite got was - what the hell was she thinking? A girl's school? And yes, to add to the danger I was a bit of a mummy's boy too. Why the danger? Bear with me. Anyway, there was I, little me, 4 years, 8 months and 10 days old. In a girl's school. Never let it be said that boys of 4 years, 8 months and 10 days don't realise how strange that is. Did I say I was a mummy's boy? Never so much as looked at a goose, let alone said boo to one.

"So much better. Sarah, my daughter, she's so happy there. Hmmm, yes."

"So... why...?"

"Oh it's just right, isn't it? So much... um... safer. Better"

"Er, yes..."

I was looking down at the sand, for the most part. And there was someone else there who seemed to be there for the same reason. Blonde little girl.

All I remember is the sandpit. And the bank with the pine trees. And the blonde girl. That's it.

So why? Why me? What was it about me that had to be so different?

I've heard since about other lone boys sent to convents or other hemmed in, secluded joints. Usually the son of a teacher or priest or some such. But I, I was the son of inoffensive, normal (well, sort of) peace-loving, tax-paying middling middle-class types who had neither taught nor taken holy orders. Yes we were just nice, middling englanders. A dad, mum and three children. Slightly eccentric. With silly nicknames.

Of course we had nicknames!

Dad - he was Da.

Sarah - she was Rah, or Rat.

Josephine - Seph or Sephie.

Peter, that's me. Groo. Don't ask.

And Mum. Well Mum was just Mum. To everyone.

Rat went to Lesley House. Lesley House was the annexe of Bankton High on the other side of town. It was in a rather grand late Georgian house with a beautiful garden. Rather kindly Headmistress. More like a dowager aunt than a Head. Very

Anne of Green Gables. If I'm completely honest, I wouldn't have minded going there. Very cosy, very safe and you got lots of attention. But then I was living in a matriarchy. Almost.

Sephie was still young. There was no educational challenge there. She was barely out of nappies. Wasn't even getting the Mrs. Youde treatment yet.

Mrs. Youde, by the way, was the best ever play school teacher. Ever. She owned a nursery school just off Widcombe Hill. She looked after the nice young things. It was all very Joyce Grenfell. Lilting voices, scraping chairs, piano music (from somewhere - I can never quite remember). Malted biscuits, milk, elevenses, taken at 11 on the dot. Telly - "Play School", exclusively. Perennially floral - hydrangeas, wisteria, lilacs, hardy roses - long thin garden outside, with blue swing and pink slide. Potato prints and the smell of PlayDough. That's where I'd been. That's where Seph went too, afterwards.

Yes, nursery school was easy. No controversy. Posh it might have been, to a fair extent. But it was as safe as Bathonians' Georgian houses, uncontroversial, professional as they came and really rather good.

So why That School? Why the school in the middle of the steep hill on the other side of town?

Well, there was the 'C' word, of course. Comprehensives to you. For Mum, the new State School system was asking for trouble. Wreaking havoc on decent people with their regard for form, structure and The Right Thing To Do. It showed complete disregard for tradition, hierarchy, merit and attainment. Everything good, in other words. She knew she was right. She could see it from those grubby kids who went to St. John's.

Even then I could sense she'd got it wrong.

But then Mum wasn't just reacting to the local education system. She was becoming disillusioned with the whole shebang.

Bath was not after all the centre of all things bright and beautiful. This was Bath in the late sixties and she hadn't reckoned on all those lovely little shops in Southgate Street being about to be waylaid and replaced with a new shopping mall. Whatever one of those was. Plus (and there was no getting away from it) the modern bit near the cinema was hideous - a monstrosity. In any case, Bathstone seemed to weather badly and everything was getting a little, well, black.

The people were a bit rude, too. Up themselves, pompous or brash or both.

These things bugged her and they influenced her. The current state of education, Paradise Lost, the people. Lack of trust in a host of things, I suppose

So a private school, from day one, it would have to be. And as there were no private schools for 4-year-old-onwards boys and girls within sensible reach, Sarah's school would be the choice. In any case, it was really rather good. The Lesley House version, in particular, was top notch.

The only problem was that Lesley House would not take boys in Kindergarten. So that was that. Off to the big version Peter would go - the other side of the city.

Girls for Peter for the first 3 years of his schooling. Then we would see.

Why me?

I had everything but I had love mostly. Over-generous love, perhaps. It was all-consuming. Maybe the decision was made mostly because Mum just couldn't let the precious boy out of her womb. Smother him in feminine love for as long as possible. What was for sure was that it was all Mum's decision in the end and no one else's. Mum made the decisions in our nice but dotty family and Dad went along with them for the most part. He was the bread-winner and she should spend the bread.

So Mum's idea to send me to that school was one built on her own politics, love and protection. But mostly love.

Send me to a school because it's safer. Send me to a school because the education's better, the reputation solid, according to the mores and prejudices of the time anyway. Who can blame her? Very shrewd in fact, no?

Except that it might have seemed slightly odd that I would be the only boy. Where were all the other boys whose mothers were as reasoned and as sensitive as mine? They can't ALL have been less clever, shrewd and prudent? Could they?

Why me?

I would have taken the battering that a State primary might have (but probably wouldn't have) dealt me. I could even have avoided the Canal bullying that came from the St. John's and Beechen Cliff kids when I was a few years older.

But there it was. The decision was made. And as savvy and sorted as I was at four years, 10 months and 20 days there was no way I could have been expected to have counter-uttered, "Sending me to THAT school? Not on your Nelly".

They wouldn't have listened anyway.

The School sat high on a steep hill, one of seven surrounding the once magnificent city, once the English Rome. It was peppered along Lansdown Crescent, the slightly shabbier, obscured relation of The Royal Crescent, situated a little lower down Lansdown Hill. Despite its relative obscurity, Lansdown Crescent was and still is quite splendid, with its grand 4-floored terraced houses, lording it over Bath's landscape.

It was difficult to work out where the main entrance was, for peppering reasons. It was, in fact, located inconspicuously, on the West side of Lansdown Hill. Enter that way and there really wasn't that much to notice. It was an early Edwardian, formless building with the usual odour of ammonia and slightly rancid linoleum pervading its corridors. Enter by the back gate however and it was a different story. Intricate wooded pathways, leading to constantly flowering rockeries, a deep green bank with overbearing pines at the top. Walking tentatively down towards the open aspect of the bank that led to the incongruous teaching block (more a slab, actually), I remember that smell, the fantastic lemon-y smell of the rough green leaved plant – lemon balm, I think it was. Why did that smell mean so much? It wasn't just the lemon. It was the combination of fresh moist air, lavender, lemon. And maybe it wasn't just the smell. It was the noise that came with it. Chirps, whistles, then the slightly menacing noise of girls, young and older in the background - the finish, the sheen, the lid.

The green banks led on to more fields and on and on into the distance, so it seemed, to somewhere intensely countrified. It felt, even to an infant, ancient. Maids and urns and wells and wooden settlements from 300 years ago.

Of course, when you're 4 years, 10 months and 20 days, when you first take in something like this, you don't really register it all. Not completely., though you are affected by it. You can feel it. And it's more the associated memories. Like music in Assembly - the sound of the very young, of innocence perhaps - and how it fitted perfectly with its surrounds. Or leaving school early, as we all did in that first year, getting back in time for Listen With Mother or Mary, Mungo and Midge. Or Mr. Benn. The funny thing is, it's never wonder or awe I remember. It was a stranger feeling. Like a calming drug, a fleeting moment of happiness. Bliss, as they used to say. Probably bliss.

So you didn't admire the views or take photos of or paint the flora and fauna and wonder at its colour and shape or try to record its sounds or bottle its smells, despite the teachers' best efforts. You just lived there for a while and absorbed it, like a sponge, absorbed its feminine culture.

That's one of the main reasons why, to this day, I have a strangely intense relationship with the opposite sex. It's the same sense of calm, ease but also vague excitement and, I guess, distrust of that school environment and what was captured within it that has remained so firmly embedded, forever associated with females, wherever and whenever.

CHAPTER 2

Petite paranoia and claiming a stake

So that is how it felt in the first few days, then fleetingly from then on. The air consumed you, that mild drug, encouraging your passiveness, your calm, your listlessness.

Maybe not quite so much, that second day.

Because the second day is where my story starts, properly.

The first day went off uneventfully. By which I mean I don't remember it.

Second day.

In which Peter gets lost. Not for the first time.

There were lots of us. It was morning break, down by a large rockery surrounded by a crescent-shaped path. I found myself in amongst a large group of chattering girls, all of whom seemed to be much older than me. There were maybe 200 of them. It was like we'd assembled for a large aerial shoot, like I'd seen many times on telly. Lots of kids shouting and looking up. Except there were no cameras and no-one else was there except us girls.

I stood there. Motionless. Expressionless. And then. Then I started to feel a little uneasy, then unsettled, then giddy. First experience of Crowd Terror.

All the girls started to pair off. You're a girl, I'm a girl. You're a girl, I'm a girl. You're a b... You're a girl, I'm a girl. Etcetera. They began to skip, danced even, in unison, up around the rockery. Then they seemed to speed up, defiantly moving away from the alienboychild.

The line grew and grew. It began to take on a life of its own, curling and whirling, completely in sync, monstrous, snake-like, celebratory, unstoppable.

I followed, un-paired - mesmerised, terrified. Infant paranoia had paralysed my untainted mind and I slowed right down. The Girlserpentia now wiggled off into the distance, towards 1B block and up, up, ever upwards and onwards and on again into Big School.

The play areas were now deserted. I had no idea where I was or where I was supposed to go next. And so I did what any sensible alien does when he's on deserted ground. I sobbed. Really sobbed. It had to be sobbing otherwise noone would have heard me. And sobbing's so much more effective than wailing. Wailing's a sign of acute attention-grabbing, whereas sobbing pulls at the heartstrings, makes you friends for life. Well, friends for the next 10 minutes at any rate, enough to make your little 4 year 10 month 21 days self feel himself again.

One minute of sobbing. It's all it takes. One minute. That's all. Before the cavalry comes. Or perhaps that's the infantry. Cadettes. In the perfect forms of Lucinda and Caroline.

I have to say that I fell in love immediately. Before they even started to say anything. No, maybe it wasn't love but it was certainly something quite different from what I'd felt towards my sisters. Ever. This is what happened the first time. And it happened again many, many more times with many, many more girls, young and not-so-young.

They genuinely looked concerned. I tell you, if you're 4 years 10 months and 21 days old, sobbing works.

"Who's this?" says Caroline. "It's a boy. It's a boy".

Says Lucinda, "It really is. It's a little boy. What are youuu doing here?"

Yes, yes it was that kind of girls' school. Bit posh.

"Are you crying?"

"Yes."

"Are you lost?"

"Yes."

"I'm Caroline"

"I'm Lucinda"

"We're friends. Are you in Kindergarten?"

"Yes"

"I've got a brother. He's not here. He's at King Edward's"

"Don't cry. We'll look after you."

And off we trotted. Probably. Through the door of 1B Block. Where I was dispatched, barely embarrassed, to my fellow gels.

And that was that. My induction. I needed a trick or two. And that was a trick I repeated. A few times. Worked a treat.

So I learnt from early on, from being lost and bewildered. If you're going to be a boy at a girl's school, be a girl.

CHAPTER 3

Autumn 1969: Peter, what's it like to be a Little Prince?

So from then on I was there and it was completely normal. Normally complete. I don't really remember any more feelings of even the slightest unease for at least another year. In retrospect, it was even better than that. I think, for the first and quite possibly the only time in my life, I was being mollycoddled by outsiders. The perfect extension to the family nest.

So, for example. When I'd been there perhaps a month, when Mum came to pick me up, she found a little boy, sitting on a bench next to the coat-racks, with legs outstretched. One girl sat, or possibly lay, crouched by each foot and gently (though with not a little effort) put one of his shoes on. "Here's your shoe, Petey". Another was positioned, exactly as the first girl, exactly opposite her. She put the other one on. They were like the two porcelain King Charles Spaniels guarding the hearth in the Sitting Room. As he stood up and stretched his arms out and up, another girl stood on the bench and lifted his coat down over his arms and body, after which a fourth stood opposite him and lovingly buttoned it up.

I'd made my move early, you see, made my mark.

The teachers were falling in too.

It all began with Reading.

Why do I remember those books more than the maths books?

Possibly because they were Rainbow Books. Starting at red, finishing at violet. A perfect goal to aim at.

The red books you wrote and drew in.

Beautifully simple. In order to read best you interacted with your book.

So the first page, I think, was one word. "Me". Existential book, slightly controversial. Read Me. Then write Me. Then draw a picture of Me.

I couldn't draw. Not then, not now, not ever, not really. But it's probably true to say that that first drawing in that first red book was as good as it got. I was ready to read and I was ready to write. Drawing was something I already did, so for some reason that didn't seem to be part of this statement of intent. So it got ignored forever.

Next page was, naturally, two words. "A house". Read a house, write a house, draw a house. Best house I ever drew, too. Not quite as good as Me but close.

That book still has a special place. It represents one of my very few stakes in the ground, perhaps my one and only successful partnership with conformity, a time when life was truly free from perversity.

It also sent out a winning signal. "You gave me these books. I'm gonna get through them. Gonna be first to the finishing line." Being competitive was never obnoxious then. No boasting, no bragging, no bullying. Just impulsive, compulsive. You felt like winning, you tried to win, you won. Simple.

So they gave me those books. I devoured them.

There were three of each colour. Red books were the slowest, mostly because of the drawing and writing of course. From Yellow onwards you didn't interact. Strange perhaps but it seemed to work. Not many words on the page but it definitely meant a progression, definitely meant growing up. And feeling like you're growing up was important then. Another little rung on the ladder, getting closer to the bigger people. Loved the Orange books. Orange was my favourite colour. Actual stories began in Orange. Usually about boys and girls in houses, getting dressed, having breakfast, going to school. As the books progressed through the spectrum the stories got less parochial, more exotic. And, of course, the writing got smaller.

By the time I got my specs, in June 1970, I'd got to Green. The following year, same time, end of Violet. Then came true splendour. Bronze, Silver and Gold. The stories were involved, fabulous. Foreign lands, unfamiliar places, landscapes. Stories of roaming across the desert or Life in a Big City. Or something like that. Of course I was more concerned with getting to the finishing line than the stories themselves. So that by the time it all happened, in February 1972, momentous as it was, I'd done with reading. Well, fiction at any rate. Maybe for another 10 years. As long as that. From then on it was Pears Cyclopedia, Guinness Book of Records, Comics, History of Film. Facts. Stuff about attainment, about success.

After a month or so, not only had I mastered Me, My House, My Garden, a trip to the butchers and possibly two pints of milk, I'd worked the territory too.

There I stood, The Little Prince. With Harem thrown in.

But at what price? Oh well, if you're going to go down, you might as well go down with a fight and enjoy it while you're there.

Mum just stood there awestruck. This was better than even she'd imagined. So suited Peter's character. Absolutely ideal for early progress.

And God only knows what it would've been like had he gone to one of those nasty State Primaries.

And that was that. Institutionalised. In cotton wool and feathers. Condemned by candyfloss.

CHAPTER 4

The Party

Early on that first term we had the first party. And as luck would have it, that party was my own. Naturally it cemented my soaring reputation as Boy About Girlsville.

It was the weirdest party of course.

Weirdest in the best kind of way. Weirdest mostly in retrospect. Because it was also at the time, in retrospect, the best party I've ever had. And I've had some corkers!

Everything was like it was in the books. Well, one in particular. It was a Ladybird book. Called The Party. Almost as good as Tootles The Taxi.

These books really were *that* good. We experience like adults, we feel like children, when you're a child. Trite and cheesy to an adult, a parent maybe but to a small child the taxi's his friend. For real. That taxi's a good-hearted, fun, cheery taxi. Helpful too! It was those big eyes for headlights - "headleyes"!

I'm convinced a small child readies itself, for life, through rhymes and stories. The Party took me through the steps for preparation perfectly. There was the trip to the shops, first of all. The ironmongers, the fishmongers, the grocers. Then the... No, hold on, maybe that was Shopping with Mother - another cracker. Anyway, the boy got ready, and the girl got ready, simultaneously in separate rooms, dressed in perfect clothes. Cute, romantic even. She had an exquisite little dress and he, he had buckled shoes! I had buckled shoes too. They were patent leather and flipping horrible. But, for a little while, they were perfect too, just like in the book. Then the kids in the book played instantly memorable games. Like Farmer's in the Den. Definitely. I remember. It was Farmer's in the Den.

So, it was set up, My Party. The little people came in, deposited their presents, one-by-one. The Beatrix Potter book. The Blue Peter annual. The felt tips. The crayons. The toy cars. Dinky and matchbox. Then there was the perfect start to the perfect party. Musical Bumps. Followed by Pass-The-Parcel. Followed by Musical Chairs. Then What's the Time Mis-ter Woo-ulf. We really did play these games, this wasn't just in the book. Then we had Perfect Tea. Hedgehogs with bits of pineapple, cheese and all that. Smiths Crisps in abundance. Oodles of orange squash. Club Biscuits - orange AND raisin. Think we had Sausages on sticks. Sausages on sticks made me sick. That came later though. Jelly - all colours and flavours. Then Da would horse around, pulling faces and telling funnies and the children would laugh a lot. Then we'd set up the projector and watch some rented cine film. Think it was Thunderbirds. Thunderbirds and Disney cartoons. I can still smell the musty whiff of the projector screen. Loved that smell. Then we'd have a couple more games - Blind Man's Buff and Musical Statues, Farmer's In The Den to end it all. Then "thanks for my present. Bye-bye."

Perfect, then.

The only thing was this.

There's a photo somewhere. I have a look at it from time-to-time. Every time I get the unnerving feeling that it's not actually true. It didn't happen. That some joker somewhere decided to comp a picture of a toothless little boy surrounded by little girls. A lot of girls. What makes it real though is that I'm the only one actually looking at the camera. That makes it real. It's like I'm saying "Isn't *this* fun! Me. Me, surrounded by pretty girls. Me, the centre of it all. The Farmer's in the Den. With not one wife but 20. Bet you don't have this at YOUR school."

Odd. Totally odd. It made complete sense at the time. But then I didn't know that girls will be girls and boys... well...

Oh those parties were great. Flippin' marvellous, the lot of them.

Zarah Dunkley. She had a good one. Her dad was brilliant. What a host! Constantly entertaining. Never stopped. Funny how the best Dads make the best parties.

There were those packets of multicoloured felt-tips you used to win as first prize. Or second. Don't think I actually won the first prize. Or did I? Anyway, at Zarah Dunkley's party they'd devised a treasure hunt. Their house was out in Bradford-upon-Avon. Think it must have been an old mill or something. You had a lot of that sort of thing out there. It was amazing. All these rooms that interlinked. Think they had a clown as well. Or maybe it was a magician. Maybe it was both.

Then there was Sarah. And Jane. And Judy. And Catherine. Remember Catherine's in particular as it was up in Coombe Down, in her Dad's vicarage. Or maybe that was Judy's Dad. Maybe he was the vicar. And Catherine's Dad was Mr. Spear. Spear's Sausages. Anyway, the Vicarage was something else. And visiting it was something else too.

All the houses were big. And old. With character. And all the parents were warm and welcoming. And didn't seem to think it odd at all that there was only one boy invited.

There really was a lot of love in those parties. Parties sealed relationships. You kind of felt loved by the parents too, even though you barely saw most of them.

Love wasn't a smothering thing. It wasn't a pat-on-the-head thing either. Love was just there, warm, constant. People were friendly - they seemed to know who you were and why you were special. The girls were no different. They were special too. I always remember one in particular coming in to the Present Room at the beginning of my party. Jane Bacon. Don't know why it was her in particular but I always remember a kind of silent, very respectful affection as she passed me my Blue Peter Annual 1969. Same with her mum. That was real friendship, I think it was. It was warm, sincere, loving. Taintless.

The kind of pure friendship never attained in adulthood.

A PTTV PRODUCTION

Going to School

Welcome... to Going to School. I'm Peter.

It's Monday. It's sunny.

Through the gate at the top and down the path.

Look at the trees. And the girls. And the teachers.

That's Judy, that's Catherine. There's Deborah. Hello! We'll be back after the break.

Welcome back.

We're in the lower school block now. The newer bit. I've turned, er, left, no right, no left. We're just going down this dippy bit, to the loos. And the smell. It's not wee or poo. It's something else. I think it's what they use to clean the wee and poo. Or maybe to cover the smell of the wee and poo. I like looking at the row of small loos, with their white bottoms and black lids. They're so small. I think they're funny.

It's also funny that I like that smell. Don't you?

It smells a bit like when we do art. When I look at our silly faces, trees and suns, that's like what I smell. Look! That's what's happening in there! That's Transition. That's where I'll be next year. That's Mrs. Thompson. She's nice. I think she's nice all the time.

And there - that's 1B. That smells of piano and drumsticks. I'll be there in 2 years. That's miles off. There's Miss Higgins. She takes assembly a lot. That's where we sing hymns and where Miss McKay is a lot. Miss Higgins is nice. She's round. She's old.

And here we are in Kindergarten. That's where I am. It smells of Mrs Ponting. She's nice. She thinks I'm a good reader. Sometimes she smacks.

And there's Catherine and Judy again. And Zarah. And Jane.

I'll introduce you to some of the older girls later. Anyway, we'll be back again on Monday, where we'll be outside, in the garden, playing games and telling stories. See you on Monday. Bye bye.

CHAPTER 5

Nuture & Nurture

It was all so soft, that first term. Soft, dreamy.

It was so soft, you didn't even finish the day. You stopped in the middle of the day and went home.

Sitting with Mum. Sitting with Mother, Listening With Mother. And Watching.

There's that piece of music. Faure, I discovered later. Dolly Suite. Shut your eyes... and you're three. Or four. Or five. Keep them shut. There's that music. Listen. Forget about the twee, forget about Middle Classness. Just listen. Just two pianos. An accompaniment, up and down again. Then the octave-spaced notes for the melody. Just plaintive and very economical. Very simple and perfect, for a child.

And when you hear it again, you're still a child. Because you are, really. All your life.

So Faure, and Auntie, knew what they were doing in the Golden Days of Radio. Days I just about managed to grab the end of. A Little Light Music for the Little Masses.

Occasionally I'd listen to The Archers. And Women's Hour. With the Book Reading at the end. Always the Book. Like the Book at Bedtime. Except for Ladies. And Girlies. Like me.

Or else there was telly. Mid-day telly.

Nothing can quite describe the fond familiarity of music and pictures, designed to evoke expectation, excitement and happiness. It's something so difficult to recapture once you're over 10.

It really didn't matter whether it was Andy Pandy, The Wood-entops, Trumpton, Chigley, Pogles Wood, The Herbs, Mary, Mungo & Midge or Mr. Benn. The atmosphere on that 22" screen was palpable. You felt something, you really did. You had no idea it was a clarinet that was making you feel something un-identifiable yet special, any more than you knew that it was a wooden figure that had been gently pushed into position thou-sands of times before you saw it, come to life for your pleasure on screen.

What I loved most of course was the "set up". A lifelong ob-session began there and then with the opening of things - the start, the renewal. New school, new town, new lover, new part-ner, new job, new country. The opening credits.

Sound and vision. From the glockenspiel Watch with Mother Flower, to the Trumpton guitar and town hall clock, then the Mary Mungo & Midge town and organ-woodwind band, the Mr. Benn wheel - like the girl, the dog and the mouse but with xylo-phone. Fresh openings, one, at least, a year. All magic, all per-fectly concocted, just for me.

But then there was Joe.

These were, after all, the days of Modern. And even pre-school tots had to face the future. Sometimes, of course, the future was bleak. Sometimes, the future was Joe. Joe was probably a bit much for a sensitive cotton-woolly like me. Joe was an only child. On his own. Lived in a transport caff. Life looked lonely for Joe. Plus the music was rubbish. It twinked and it twonked and it moved too quickly for a lonely boy. And Joe didn't move much at all. He wasn't pushed or had his strings pulled. He Just stood there in his dungarees, looking pretty, 'till the next frame. He required more concentration as well as the ability to appre-ciate that there were lovely young boys, the same age as me, who were much worse off than I. And I couldn't. Appreciate, that is. He was just a picture who didn't move much. A picture of a boy who just stood there, 'till the next picture appeared.

A lonely boy. On his own.

On the other hand.

Maybe I should have taken Joe in a bit more. After all, his Mum, who seemed very kind, loved him and so did his Dad, who was funny. And he was being taught to be independent - to think and do for himself.

And I - well, I was continually nurtured, not natured, by what seemed to be an eternal matriarchy and its maternal offspring.

I should have been more Joe. And worn dungarees.

CHAPTER 6

Spring 1970: Not in front
of the children

It's so easy to blame your parents. For everything. Your views because of when they turn on you and conspire against you, make you unpopular. Your love life. Because they were who they were and they forced you to be who you are. Your career. They felt a failure so should you. Your moods. And the rest.

Sometimes it's all too easy to pass blame. And when you think about it, my career couldn't have been more different from my parents'. So maybe we should all move on.

That they were an influence though is undisputed.

Mum was a well-to-do, unlike Da. So you'd have thought that a place like Bath would have suited her. But in Bath it was difficult to be yourself.

I remember now.

We were picking up Rah from school at Lesley House. Mum and I were chatting about her best friend Audrey, I think. I would have been 5. Mum's friends in Bath were never "Aunty" for some reason.

"Audrey's got Ray at home so we can't go for our coffee morning tomorrow after all. Which is a real shame, Groo, as she says she has some news and has picked up a Georgian trinket for me in Bristol. I really wanted…"

Pause.

"Mum?"

"I…er…"

"What, Mum?"

A plump woman approached, rose complexion, dogtooth suit, white silk scarf blowing whimsically, somewhat haughty-looking seven year old girl in tow. They seemed to be looking somewhere in our direction though it was difficult to discern any expression of engagement. Both of them looked casually hurried, if such a thing were possible.

Mum snorted. Well maybe not snorted… just, well, hmphed.

"Hmph"

Nothing. Not a snotty dicky bird from the intended.

Then she hrrhed.

"Hrrh"

And as they sauntered past, I remember feeling slightly soiled.

I'm sure neither Mum nor Rah barely knew either of these people, Minor Miss or Major Moddom. She certainly didn't have to acknowledge them. I think though that she had been cast under a rather uncomfortable spell. Or rather outcast. She suddenly felt an itchy need to ingratiate, partly due to her harmonious nature and in part to her desire to up-woman herself. In retrospect, Dogtooth hadn't done anything seriously anything, other than project herself in an upturned manner. Mum could have turned the other cheek of course. There's no doubt that The Elevated One intended every atom of discomfort she caused.

Mum might have had another, more feisty view, of course, which would no doubt have passed sweetly along like this -

"What are you looking at?"

"I'm sorry?"

"What are you looking at, Snooty Knickers?"

"I'm afraid I have no idea what you're…"

"Oh yes, very good! You think you can come at me with your airs and your look-at-me-hoity-toity? Do you? Well, do you?! Would you like to tell me exactly what right, if any, you have of protruding your snivelling little nose into the air like that when decent people like me and my son are just gaily going about our business in your proximity, like any other decent neighbour might? Or are you going to pass by flouncily with your flatulent fat arse and your snivelling sidekick? You're contaminating the air, Missis Fartypants, simple as that. If I ever catch you fouling it up again in my presence, I'll reach for my bag, so I will and the least you can expect is a [pause for dramatic effect] *sore* protruding hooter and flabby derri-aaaier".

But the spell had had its effect and Mum was reduced to a hmph.

This particular specimen belonged to a popular coven of witch Mum was neither member nor even aware. And as much as I felt for her, it was these types who turned her into someone almost as precious. Though not nearly as bitchy.

There were other factors.

She'd always liked the affectations of life, for sure. Or maybe it wasn't really that. She liked to think that culture was high and low. And that high was what you aspired to. So it was Mozart and Schubert for her. George Eliot. Les Liaisons Dangereuses. Even light entertainment had to be a little haute. Call My Bluff. Face the Music. It was only us dear children who brought things down to earth a little with Dick Emery, The Two Ronnies (Mum liked these), Morecambe and Wise (she didn't like these) and The Diddy Men (she hated these). For her, "Dishy" was usually a Shakespearean actor or classical musician. Her favourite was an Australian actor well known for his portrayal of Abelard and Henry VIII. And not so well known for his cheesy (though surprisingly appealing) renditions of easy listening songs of the day.

And Bath brought out the very worst of her in terms of what you might call high culture consumables. Shopping at Caters, Bath's equivalent of Fortnums, for example. Or getting stocked up with Jaeger jackets. Granted that she could rarely afford to buy that sort of stuff. For some reason it just had to be like that for her. Stylish low-rent didn't exist in those days. Marks 'n' Sparks was all you got and you made good in that department. In any case, everyone knew that their stuff was grimly un-stylish - even when you were 5. Pants being an exception of course.

Dad went along with her, to some extent, just to keep the peace. He had a certain sartorial lack of anything going on in the couture department. "Dishevelled Prof" was his look. He'd smartened up a little since the days of the docks but he was still reluctant. Eventually he was persuaded to buy a half-decent suit. So he'd be forced down to Austin Reed where there'd be a nice Harris tweed number. Actually that was a pretty cool suit, as it turned out. I dug it out when I was sixteen. It lasted for five whole years. Until I sizzled it against a three-bar fire in Manchester.

And he liked the occasional posh meal out. In those days there wasn't much choice anyway.

He did it all for her in any case.

His biggest sacrifice, by a Brooklands mile, had been cars. Once his wheels were swingin', even decadent. He once left a white Jag he'd bought "just for the holiday" in a Southern French lake - how dreadfully cool was that! That was about as far away from Da as I could possibly imagine. "Careful with money" would be a seriously diplomatic understatement. Perhaps he changed his spendthrift nature once he'd met Mum. Perhaps her anchoring put a padlock on his purse because as soon he and Mum were married he downgraded. So Mum got a Hilman Minx 1965 (sort of "posh mummy"), followed by a Triumph Herald (almost groovy), then a Cortina and a Morris Mini Minor Traveller. The Cortina was grey-blue with that weird cold plastic seating (also grey-blue). Horrid, nasty car. The other things about nearly all family cars of the day were how nearly all of them were cramped. Even the big ones. So all three of us would be squeezed into the back of the Cortina like sardines. The Mini was a bit more fab as, if you were good, you got to travel in the boot.

While Mum's procession of cars were downwardly mobile, Dad's were utterly nondescript. A reflection on how he now saw his life - functional at best. He started with a Renault 8, slightly nice as it had sticky-out wing mirrors, perched - like they were in those days - on top of the headlights. Next came trundling a Peugeot 204. The French Lada. Think he had a few of those.

Mum's parking was legendary.

"I wonder if I can see a… ah, there's one". The customary 18 foot space - longer by 2 feet than a regulation parking bay these days - greeted us with a broad smile. The Hillman was 13 feet long.

Mum was one of those Mums who took to driving relatively late in life. She'd passed her test not 5 years before at the tender age of 41. They say that you need one driving lesson for each year of your life. I think Mum must have had over 60. The first test inspector ran for the hills. The next seven needed immediate attention from their colleagues - nearly all of them upped their medication I think.

She was fairly unaware of the road. Luckily for her, Bath's traffic flow was benign so, largely because of habitual repetition, her driving did improve.

But not her parking.

The parking space waited patiently. "Now, I must remember… ok, right, now! We're there. Hold on…"

The Hillman / Cortina / Mini was automatic. The Herald was not. It took Mum just 6 months to burn its gearbox out. I don't think I ever heard of anyone since who's managed to do that.

"OK. Here we go. Hello, how are you? Yes, I'm fine. See you inside? Oh - you're going to Boots. Yes, see you on Thursday."

"Mum?"

"What? Ah, yes. Hold on"

The first horn hoots.

"Hold on! Now then, here we go"

Mum turned the wheel vigorously ot the left, pulled it round three times, then put her left foot on the clutch and took a deep breath, After lifting her foot slowly (I counted to 10 before the bite) turned the steering wheel vigorously to the left, then tentatively then slowly The back of the But she always got there. Got quite good, ultimately. These were the days before multi-storey car parks. You had car parks of course, on one level, but you could also park on the road. Because in those days most of the shops had the decency to hang out on the High Street.

I have to say that other family members', in particular Rah's, reflections on Mum's driving didn't influence me. I never felt unsafe. I think I must have been wrapped in a divine cloak.

Sainsburys was in Southgate Street. You parked right next to it if you had a small car, which Mum's were for the most part. She'd shimmy her way in, feeling quite flushed with pride. Took her about 5 minutes to get in, probably more. But... Huzzah she'd got to within two yards of the entrance! And in we'd hop.

Used to love standing by the jelly aisle. There was something about the jelly in those days. You don't get it anymore. Strawberry in particular I remember. They say that the senses bring out memories or other associations but I just can't see how at that age it would have done that. I certainly don't remember it sparking anything else. All I know is that I was completely static, packet in hand, breathing deeply. It was my catnip. Then there were the queues. Don't happen anymore. Queues were an interesting way to make friends, if you could be bothered, because you'd be there for as long as an hour. The tills were proper manual things, not those pretend thingies you get now. Proper tills with buttons with different amounts on and everything. That's why it took so long - cashier punching each item in. Queues would typically stretch the length of the aisle.

At Sainsburys you'd load up the boxes into the car. Plastic bags didn't exist. Life was more recyclable in those days. Boxes (I liked the ones that had been used to pack Puffa Puffa Rice) were the thing. I learned fairly early on how to do the best pack. After a while I could even carry the smaller ones out of the car, into the house. Proper shopper!

At Caters though it was different. Caters was posh. You didn't take the boxes with you. You didn't even pack. You had it delivered. It was a sign. A sign of haute breeding. Lorry would come down that oh-so-narrow drive, driver would get out, muttering mostdisgustingexpletives, sweating buckets, haul the boxes in, mutter evenmoredisgustingexpletives, almost back into the flower bed, take 20 minutes to negotiate the backing manoeuvre, back and forth, back and forth he'd go, then finally wheeze up the drive back to sanity.

Mum loved the High Life. Boxes from Caters weren't the only delivery. Laundry came rattling down the drive too. Bolloms. Every week. Nice pristine sheets. Blankets occasionally. Shirts too of course, as appropriate.

But the ultimate in High Life for Mum, was the hairdressers. The Salon. 70s High Life - Italian Style. Time was when all hairdressers of a certain ilk and hautery were all Italian. They must have been. This particular salon was called Franco's. Franco had a brother, called Scarzino. Or Scarpino. They also had another brother who was the black sheep. Federico.

Mum's favourite. And her favourite time of the month.

"Signora. Sooo delightful to see you again."

"Oh, you too, Federico."

"Can I get you a coffee? No sugar? Caffè bianco, presto! Let me see… ah, a little bouffant, yes?"

"Yes, you've got it. With a little Federico magic, if you please."

"3 hours of wizardry coming up, Signora!"

She was in love with all of them. Because they got paid to flatter. And they did it beautifully. In Pecara Nera's case, he managed to flatter by grunting. He was a cavalier with the scissor blade, completely. And when it came to The Brush… Oh my! It was like watching an old Rudolph Valentino film. There were those lovely ladies with knee-length skirts and trim jackets, sitting underneath those weird sit-under driers, sneaking a peak from their copy of The Lady upon my Mum getting manhandled by a vigorous Italian in his mid-thirties. The groaning was palpable. James Bond with dryer for weapon of choice. And Mum - shaken and stirred.

Occasionally Mum took Sarah with her to the hairdressers for a sort of non-descript shoulder-length trim.Rah had been born with gorgeous curls and was the model of a baby and toddler. By this time - she was eight - her hair had straightened out. What's more, she'd been affected by another kind of confidence-sapping crisis.

Sarah's eyesight was poor. She'd recently been dragged along to the opthamologist and forced to wear black-framed glasses - NHS specs. I thought she was dead lucky, later when I was forced, much more cruelly I thought, to wear greeny-blue horn-rimmed spectacles for Very Ugly Boys. Anyway,Rah was not happy - in fact she was miserable. Specs just would not do. So she would take it out on her soft brother if it was the last thing she ever did. Which of course it wouldn't be. Where would the fun be in that? So she continued to pummel my sensitive little head for the next couple of years, by which time, the time when she became one of the first 10-year-olds to wear contact lenses, she'd got so used to it she kept going for at least another 10.

So persecution came early and came in the form of My Lovely Elder Sister.

Seph was too young. Much too young for me or anyone else to notice. I knew that she fibbed about stuff she'd done whatever with - like the time when she was 3 and almost convinced us that she'd eaten her boiled egg when she'd done no such thing. We found the egg in the pedal bin as it turned out but she had us going for more than a minute.

The thing is, prone as she was to big fibbing, Seph was a wee victim in all of this. In that no-one paid her the slightest bit of notice. She was numero tre, the cast-me-down, the forlorn loner. At the tender age of 2, what's more. Being born in possibly the most traumatic time of our child lives didn't help. Dad had been virtually dying of double pneumonia so Mum hadn't exactly been in the right mood to bring another darling into the world. But another had indeed been born, then taken to Dad's Deathbed for a quick screening, then swiftly off to Betty's for the end of Christmas, New Year and another couple of weeks for good measure.

No, Seph, unlike a lot of little brats, didn't do much wrong to cause her folks pain in her infancy. She just happened to be born into it - pain, that is. And remained in it for some years to come, until when, came the Glorious Day, at 16, she established her Independent Self.

And having me for a neglectful brother can't have helped much either.

So Seph's way of establishing herself in those years was to draw attention by a bit of simple divisiveness. Deviancy.

And, in retrospect, you had to feel for Sarah too, being dragged down by an envious mother, in contrast to Da who adored her, her siblings who were both good-for-nothing and having to deal with the shameful tragedy of specs to boot.

So we were all victims. Except that for me it was the simple fact that I was sandwiched between the two of them. If I'd been the youngest or the eldest then I think I would have had certain privileges. It's just that I seemed to have the worst of both worlds, as it were.

Dad was Da then. Like I was Groo. Nicknames. A family thing. Must've been a Jewish thing too. Mum liked that so she joined in too.

Da was mostly at or under things. Under the bonnet of the car, or the chassis by the wheels. Under the sink or at the washing machine. Or the wiring. Or making another table. Think he made at least two while I was at The School. Both with Formica tops. Red I think.

Nothing was exactly elegant in our house (though Da had inherited some cracking furniture and Mum had her antiques) but at least it worked. For the most part. Thanks to Da.

He used to make useless electrical apparatus. Like a tall wooden contraption which had paddles at the top (think they were from an old car, a Morris Minor) which moved up and down, like two robotic arms. No actual use for it. It just did that, that's all. It was fun. I loved it.

He once made a small electronic organ. Like a Stylophone - it was about the same size, perhaps just a little bigger, except this had buttons which you pressed and they in turn would hit contacts and make the Stylophone sound. Think I got that for my 7th birthday.

He was also a musician. You couldn't fail to be where he came from. He also had perfect pitch. Although I was never quite sure what that was I used to think that that proved he was a God-made genius. He taught himself to play the piano and would improvise pieces in the style of Bach and Mozart. "Who's that, Dad?", thinking it was Bach-y or Handel-y - like something we'd listened to on Face The Music or on the radio. "Oh, nothing. Just something I made up".

He was an artist too. He sketched Sarah beautifully a number of times. You could see his devotion in each swish of the pencil. His copying was extraordinary. He could paint in oils and pastels, as accomplished as anyone who made a living out of it.

I always used to think he'd make a great school teacher, or even prof. Even when I was little.

But then he was far too principled as well as practically minded for all that.

When I was little I was always a little scared of Da. He's someone you definitely didn't take on. Then I suppose that was fairly common for married men of his generation. They had to keep their distance. Had to concentrate on the bread-winning. Had to stick to the task in hand. "Us time" would've been frowned upon. And definitely don't share your thoughts, your fears, your demons. With anyone, and especially not with your kids.

Mum idolised him. I think that's fair to say. He was her saviour. And she treated him that way.

While I was at The School (and for some time after) we never had tea with Da. Our tea was earlier, at about 5. His was about 7:30, as soon as he'd got home from work.

We all used to think he worked very, very hard. I think that's because that's what Mum said. I think he did, though perhaps it was made worse than most by the fact that he drove nearly 60 miles every day.

These days I guess, living for the most part in a big city, I don't think much about travelling to work for an hour each way every day, something I've done all my life.

In those days and for Da I think it did make a difference. These were narrow roads, for most of the year travelled through in the dark. Cars weren't as luxurious and as smooth as they are now. Da would usually start work about 8, which meant he left at 7.

The other thing was that Da didn't really like his work. It was fairly miserable. After the successes of his work in the sixties, he'd put his ambitions as well as his emotions behind him and now worked in the electronics division of a company based in Stroud in Gloucestershire. The company made parts for industrial machinery, I think. Though he never really told us. Don't think he wanted to. There was a bit of him that was too ashamed. Union activity was fairly non-existent at work - the bosses had seen to that and it was the first place he'd worked in where he'd felt entirely powerless, I think. To be honest I never really knew as he never really said anything about what he felt. I pieced all that stuff much later on, at the time of his Illness. In any case, it was a Generation Thing. Not many men expressed themselves in those days. It wasn't just selflessness. It's just that they never saw the point. I think that's what did for him in the end.

Not that Da behaved miserably for a lot of the time. Like a lot of Jewish men he had a finely tuned funny bone. And he was one of the most appealing people I'd ever met. And also one of the most embarrassing. At family dos, let's say at Betty's, his voice was the loudest - I realised later that's why he'd been such an effective Union representative. Whenever anyone got up to make a speech (which they usually did, the number of 50ths and 60ths we went to), his was the heckler's voice. I think it's because he was particularly un-fond of pomposity, having been witness to it so much whilst he was growing up.

The kids (particularly young kids) loved him. He'd do funny voices most of the time. Goonish voices, usually posh gits. He was a fantastic mimic. That perfect pitch thing again. It meant he could do Yorkshire and Lancashire just like t'natives. It was funny that his favourite film was "I'm Alright Jack", not exactly the most real representation of the struggle between Workers and factory owners. It's just that humour always won for him in the end.

The other thing that I found a bit odd growing up was how much he loved France. I think he must either have worked in France in the fifties or knew some French people in Liverpool (a young woman, perhaps - that would've been good) though I'm really not sure how that could have been. We went to France a couple of times, camping. Everyone thought he was French, even – particularly - the French which I found extraordinary. Must have been that gift for mimicry.

Da was just very, very warm. Almost too warm. And very loveable.

And troubled. Initially I didn't really think much of it. You get used to someone shouting "Ohhh, gerrrt onnnn wiiiith ittttt" in the car, in a queue, on the way to Betty's in Southport or Liverpool or France or somewhere or somesuch. The gritted teeth, accompanied by a low moan, then a yelp. Or a distressed, almost panicked frustration. When you're young you see these things, from your parents or someone else who's close. You absorb them, for sure. More often than not you don't really register them or dwell on them. They just exist. Like your sisters irritating habits or your Mum's snorting at relative strangers.

At the time it didn't matter so much to any of us that he was troubled. That came later.

So at that time Da was just Da. Anxious but deeply funny. A genuine eccentric. A Good Man. We loved him.

And Mum loved him the most. For years they'd brought out the best in each other. Which was just to be themselves. And the further they were from each other, the more distant they became. From themselves, from the world.

There was the mutual admiration. The energy that feeds the family, perhaps. She admired him for his humour, his eccentricities. And the fact that she'd saved him. Most importantly she admired his kind, sensitive soul. He admired her for her warmth and the fact that she was nearly always right. Of course he loved the fact that she admired him in her ways. Most men did. And do.

The bickering was their daily work out. I've never really found bickering awkward or embarrassing. It's like the birds. Mum's and Da's bickering was the dawn chorus, a reminder of the glorious chaos of life. How else were they going to work things out?

Mum, Da, Rah, Groo, Seph. The leaders, the followers. The couple, the three. The culprits. Mum the innocent slayer of all things sensible. Sisters the troublemakers and obstructions. Dad the constant entertaining outsider. All contributing to the fast-approaching smooth, gentle, surreal and perverse life of the Protagonist. Peter was done for. Yet and typically in the nicest possible way.

CHAPTER 7

1970: A House

Of course everything was connected in those days. The way I lived in The School. The way I lived in The House. Everything that happened then, wherever it was, wherever in that strange city in any case, affected me for the rest of my life.

I still dream about the house.

It wasn't a pretty house. It had that wall covering - a kind of white pebble dash - which constantly looked mucky. Constant mucking about over its 200 years life had turned it from a small cottage into a large, labyrinthine 5-bedroomed house.

But it was magnificent. Like the school, it was built on one of the seven hills. And it was surrounded by an amazing garden. Amazing. Down the rickety almost-tarmacked hill to a massive pine tree on the right. Then the drive opened out to a terrace - for perhaps the 2 cars - and the rose bed on the left. To the left and down the hill, a bank of perhaps 40 firs alongside a narrow lawn, with a beautiful little stone gazebo at one end with a bank halfway. Up to the right, an exotic yucca, then rockery, with ornamental everything, including birdbaths, gargoyles, crazy paving. Oh and the crazy paving was there too on the pathway that led up to the top garden (yes, it went on), with magnolia tree and all. And there was a vegetable garden to the left of the drive. And two garages. And a magnolia tree in the bottom garden too.

And all a bit run down.

Because it was one of those places you needed to attack with all the resources you had - money, personnel, passion, sheer hardcore physical grit - to get it all under control. It would take years before anyone really took it on. They're still working on it now, in fact.

Dad gave it his best shot but he never mastered it. I think it became his nemesis - kind of.

The rest of us didn't really care. We just used and abused. Particularly me. If I'd been any more boisterous I (and perhaps my friends) would have demolished it long before we eventually left.

One boy very nearly did.

We'd had some of Mum's Gerrards Cross bunch round. You want to know why I get so upset about Class in this country? This should help you.

You'd have thought that the posh would keep their own little darlings under wraps - whip them within an inch of their lives if they didn't conform from day one, bloody well do as they were told and woe, woe-est betide them if they ever did anything to upset anyone.

Which they did in spades when the little buggers came to stay. I think we just had the boys. There were two of them. 9 and 7. David and William. Snotty-nosed and evil as hell. William was the snide clever-arse, though fairly harmless. A solicitor now I think. Of course. David was a wee bastard. Cocky, rude and particularly destructive. Would go on to makes heaps of dosh in the Sports Promotion Business. Unsurprisingly. Only kids I've ever seen my Dad hit (well I think he hit both of them). He certainly put the fear of God into them. But that, maybe, is another story.

Anyway, Da had constructed a strange circular thing in the middle of the bottom lawn. 9 (or so) metal sheets, bashed together somehow so they stood up, with a large piece of black tarpaulin thrown over it. That, Ladies and Gentlemen, was our swimming pool. Well, wading pool. You couldn't exactly swim in it as a) it was waist-height and b) it was precisely 6 feet in diameter. But we loved it in our own sweet way and had a good splash-around whenever we could.

We also had a low-slung rockery down in the lower garden which looked, like the rest of the garden, a little shabby. Which was no excuse for what happened to it when David passed by. Well, he didn't so much pass as charge, picking up what he could find on the way and depositing it immediately into the swimming pool. Then he went back for more. Dismantling the mini-rockery, stone by stone, then chucking with such mini-venom that he caused a mini-tidal-wave. That, for me, was boy-being-boy. Archetypal, if I'd had known the word. He had brutish wasp-sting lips too, like Mick Jagger. Much preferred John. And Paul, George and Ringo for that matter.

The episode didn't make me female-vengeful however, relieved to be an adopted girl. It made me even less at ease, out there in the Real World, not within The School. Boys like David were just spoilt middle-class boys who had too much attention from their mums and neglect from their dads. It was the way of the world and still is, to a much lesser extent. But then, you see, I felt intimidated by and just a little envious of boys with freedom. Freedom just to be Alpha Boys.

Speaking of David's Mum, she was a bit of a trailblazer too. Foul-mouthed or so I thought. And it got me in hot water.

I was round at Auntie Mary's. Auntie Mary was my godmother. She lived in Salisbury. Her son was in the room.

So I said, "Tea's ready. Come on, fuck off."

"Mum! Mum! Mum! Mum!"

"What's the noise, what's the noise? Ian, you seen John. John, lovey, what's up? For goodness' sake."

"He swore. Peter swore."

"Oh, I think you misheard. Peter would never swear."

"Peter swore. Peter swore."

"Peter?"

"I didn't swear."

"There you go. Peter never lies. Never."

"But he said fuck. Fuck off!"

"John! He can't have!"

"He did. Didn't you!"

"Er... Y-Yes?"

Mary getting crimson.

"How? Why? This is..."

"What's wrong with fuck off? My Aunt Angela says it."

"It's a dreadful thing to say. You should never say that."

"But she says it all the time."

"What? In front of you?"

"Yes. Always. She's always telling William and David fuck off. She's told me fuck off. She told all of us fuck off."

"She can't have!"

"She has. She says - 'Fuck off and get your schoolgear ready', er, yes 'Get out of the swimming baths. We're leaving soon. Fuck off' and, er, 'Come on, come on, we'll be late. Fuck off.' She says that last one a lot"

"I don't care what she says. You should never say that, never. It's extremely rude. Isn't it Ian."

"It certainly is. Although I'm not sure... Perhaps she was asking them to buck..."

"It's dreadful, Ian, dreadful. Dreadful, Peter. Don't ever say it again."

So that was me told. I remember feeling shocked and ashamed but for no apparent reason. Confused.

It took some time before I finally realised what Angela had been really saying. Mind you, I wouldn't have put it past her to have slipped a bit of genuine "F" into the conversation from time to time as a coping mechanism. Those little buggers.

The air you breathe. The spaces you're in. The place you feel. The room you inhabit. The house was one thing, from the outside. Its ornateness, its shabby grandness. Then there was inside. Altogether a different story.

All the rooms felt lived in - that's for certain. There was always stuff laying around, covering just about every space and crevice, every nook and cranny.

Mum loved her antiques so they had their place - their special place. You went through the front door, where there was a narrow hall, then to the right into the Sitting Room ("living room", no and "lounge" most definitely not) and there they all were, pride of place. Staffordshire plate, porcelain powder thingies, Wedgwood this, Royal Doulton that, up above, down below and pride of place. The two King Charles Spaniels either side of the fireplace. How many homes had those wee Centurions of Taste? Furniture was fairly posh too - high back sofas, buttoned back chairs. Even Mum's smoking chair was fairly lavish. In time the furniture would acquire stains, then holes, upholstery would fall out. We weren't good at maintenance. Largely because there was so much to maintain. In the corner was the drinks cabinet. With the drinks. What do you think? Whisky, yes. Cinzano *and* Martini, of course. Sherry - a middle class house was incomplete without sherry. Both types. Harveys Bristol Cream and something a little drier. Campari - that stuff that tasted like nothing on earth - possibly mouthwash - I tried some later. The soda syphon. That was fun - particularly trying to get those CO_2

chargers into the top, then shaking and waiting for something to happen.

Essentially this was the room where Mum smoked and read and Dad went to sleep after his marathon day at work. We occasionally visited. I did spend time there with Mum when she'd picked me up from school at Kindergarten in the first term but essentially none of us spent much time there until, perhaps, the holidays.

Most of our time (well, mine at any rate) was spent in the playroom. You got there, from the sitting room, across the hall through the dining room and a strange little ante-room, turned right down a couple of steps and there it was.

Playroom is probably overdoing it. This was the Telly Room essentially and, although this would change later when we went all up-market and groovy-seventies-brown-corner-setteee, for now it was, well... hard to describe really. I think there was lino on the floor, though it might have been shabby carpet. There were two very old sofas, which were well past their peak condition and whose covers barely covered a set of moth-ridden, gaping, cavernous, stuffing-oozing holes. I can still smell their musty, wheeze-inducing dank ever-lingering odour. There wasn't much light in this room - it backed off to a bank outside the house and there was a high window which was hardly ever opened. Telly was in the corner, right-hand of the room to start with.

Needless to say, it was my favourite room in the house.

Everything seemed old in that house. The kitchen, perhaps weirdly, seemed the oldest room of all. Lino, again, and one of Dad's tables. One he'd made in the cellar. Red Formica top. Nice sturdy legs. Think he made two while we in Bath - this was the first one. Then there was the sink. Bit small. I remember Mum had the habit of putting all the cutlery in a small jug or glass with washing up liquid and water to soak them. We didn't have a dishwasher then. Much too up-market for us, though that of course came later. Hygiena (before QA) units. Cooker - stand-alone, grill, four rings, oven, functional and again, probably not big enough for a family of five. The chairs I think were the plainest of the plain functional kitchen chairs. That was it. It just felt old.

Kitchen was on the same side as the sitting room. As I said, the dining room was over the way. That was where the pianola was and the grand, 17th century dining table that had belonged to Dad's dad. I think it was 17th century. It certainly felt like it. Very dark mahogany, irregularly smooth (all those years of bees wax). My teeth marks on it, from when I was toddler though I never actually saw them. (Another bit of Mum's legendary apocrypha) Enough to seat about 8, I'd say, fairly comfortably. As a result it completely dominated the room until one bright spark (possibly Mum, possibly Sarah, possibly both) one year decided to put it across the bay window at the end of the room. That was much later. The chairs were red-backed Chippendale. Or so Mum told us, though this turned out to be slightly not-to-be-the-case when, years later, we had them valued. The Sideboard and Dresser stood across from the table. Beautiful piece of furniture and of course totally impractical. The drawers were difficult to open and the dresser just seemed to be another place for Mum to put her antique plates on. But then maybe every family in the country who ever had a sideboard and dresser did exactly the same.

For some reason the phone was in the dining room too. Strange place to put it.

Turn left out of the dining room and up the stairs. On the first, "mini-level" - I guess they'd say mezzanine now - was a small toilet - sorry - lavatory. Which is where, in my more constipated moments, I'd while away the hours picking off the polystyrene-backed wallpaper, chunk by chunk. I think the paper was that multi-coloured, circular, spongy stuff. Loved doing that. Can't believe I actually got away with it. Don't remember being in trouble for doing it. Wonder why?

Then up to the landing and immediately on the left was our bedroom. Ours as, for a while, all three of us slept there. Three beds, probably all the same size though that possibly isn't right, as was only two when I was at The School. I think, for some reason, that the carpet was red but maybe that's wrong too. Anyway, of course Sephie had the bed nearest the door, mine was in the middle and Sarah's was by the window. Same as in the car. I'd always sit in the middle. Sarah always had to sit by the window. Beds had sheets in those days. Sheets and blankets. The continental quilt, or duvet depending on which side of the bed you got out of, revolution came later of course. Not much later, in our case - courtesy of Cousin Bet - but that's another story. I got quite good at making my bed. I learnt all the nurses' folding tricks and everything. The fluffing up of the pillow. The precise folding over of blanket and sheet.

Out of our bedroom, left and right next to that room was spare room 1. Which had the highest beds of any beds I've ever known. Most of the time completely unlaid in. Except at Easter, Christmas or when Auntie Jean and Uncle Ronnie, Ann, Arthur, Bobbie, Charlie, Pam, Michael, Edie, Tony, Evelyn, Dick, Uncle Tom Cobley and all came to stay. A very refined room. Blue, I think. Mostly blue. Apparently, as I discovered later, Princess Charlotte, the Prince Regent's daughter, I think, came to stay and you could still smell her cheroots. Either that or Mum's Silk Cuts wafting up from the sitting room. Loved those beds - great for climbing up and bouncing on.

Along the landing and left and you were in Mum's and Dad's bedroom, which was "en suite", as we never said. Beautiful room. Bed pride of place of course. That bed was a "quality item" if ever there was one. I think it lasted half a century, mattress and all. The bathroom was very old style. It must have been at least thirty years old then. The bath was one of those with very round sides, I think. Not that posh - not free-standing or anything - I just remember its roundness. It was that Colonial pale green colour. We kids had a bathroom too, further down the landing, on the right and down small steps. Regulation white. The bath had very lime-y sides. I remember hours of fun in that bath playing "race the soap round the sides".

There was other space of course. Other times.

The room next to the bathroom became Sarah's room in time. For now it was the second spare room. Gerry, Geraldine, my first cousin - stayed there when she came to stay. Just one bed in the middle of a Hobbit Room. Very curved ceiling. Red carpet, I think. Dressing table with wooden mirror on wooden stand. One that pivoted back and forward. Used to play with that, pivoting back and forward, back and forward, back and forward...

I must have wasted loads of time in that house. No surprise. It had a lot in common with The School. It was the feel - the space, the hill, the flora, the fauna. It was less benign of course - the family made it so - but there was a sense of mirroring, of beauty, of quiet and calm distraction. Bath architecture and landscaping did that to you, when you were young.

The simple fact was that I was becoming used, almost benignly, to all this superficial beauty. It was unnerving though - soporific as its effect was - to be faced with it each and every waking hour. You see where I'm going here. Down the Ditch, quite willingly.

CHAPTER 8

Summer 1970: What is it about Older Girls?

I've always liked older girls. Just ask my wife.

Older girls, at 4 and 5, were bigger for a start. An inch or two at least. I was average height.

I liked that. I liked the feeling that there was a sense of control, even danger, from above. I never felt intimidated. Well, if I did I probably liked it anyway. But "intimidated" would be misleading. I liked girls who seemed to know more than me. Knew how to look after themselves. Because there was always a chance they'd look after me. At least for a few minutes. Or even seconds.

There was a girl in the year above. Frances. Pretty. Wavy hair. Cute smile. Looked like Sandra Dee. Strange but I think I had a massive crush on Sandra Dee when I was that age. They used to show Sandra Dee films on Sunday afternoon, after lunch and occasionally in the afternoons in the holidays. I think it was her, anyway. Might have been Carol Lynley. There was a film where she was the younger sister who fell in love. Lots of surf in her films as I remember. Very exotic, very romantic. She used to kiss boys a lot. I wished she'd kiss me. But that would have been strange. She would have been 30-something by now. In 1970. Which was old. And made me a little sad.

Anyway, Frances was cute, as I said. And older. Had a casual, calm dominance about her.

"Want a sweet?"

"What you got?"

"Lovehearts? Smartie? Opal Fruit?"

"Hmmm... Smartie"

"There you go"

An orange one.

That was the problem with older girls. That was always happening. Sometimes I just didn't know what to do. I just froze. Motionless boy. Mouth slightly agape. Looking slightly stupid.

And orange my favourite colour too.

She just smiled. And said "OK. See you." And she was off.

And then. There were the really big girls. The ones from up the top. The ones who came down, from time to time, with their sandwiches and their books. The ones who took it easy, up under the pine trees at the top of the bank, way up past the rockery.

There was one - Patricia I think - she was seventeen. Nine years older than my older sister. Now that was old. She thought I was amusing. The only boy in his year. She used to take the Mick.

"It's little Petra. Hel-lo Pe-tra. You're a funny girl, arentcha. Where's your dress? Your parents know your here? You sure you didn't get lost?"

Then she and the girls with her would start giggling.

The thing is, I never felt I was being bullied or that she was trying to show me up in any way. I'm not sure if she ever intended to do it. I just think she thought it was funny, that a little boy should be amongst little girls. It probably took the drudgery away from her studies. After all, she had been doing this school stuff for twelve years.

"Penelope - come here, Penny Poodle. Let me straighten your tie. I can style your hair if you like." I think, in the end, she thought I was quite cute. After a while she stopped with the wisecracks and kept it down to a smile, a little laugh and a wave. Still called me Petra though.

And then there was Fenella. Valkyrie Fenella. Fenella the Wee Fella.

Fenella was 6. Older than me by a few months. The year above. Don't know how our parents got to know each other but then you never do at that age do you?

She was Scottish. At least, her parents were. They lived up the drive, right and half-way along Lyncombe Hill. Unusual, box-shaped house, like a lot of those late Georgian Houses on Lyncombe Hill were. Impressive though. Her Dad owned the garage down the road. Or maybe her best friend's Dad did. Not sure. No, hang on, he worked for the Admiralty, like a lot of Dads did in Bath. Anyway, it was a nice house, with a breakfast room that you went down some steps to get to. Just like Cousin Bet's. Breakfast room? Well, I only remember having breakfast there, so, yes, it was the kitchen but for me it meant breakfast.

You know that moment when you can't quite seize a memory? The moment when something happens in the present that reminds you of something that probably happened decades ago but which just flashes across your lobes? Like when your eight year old daughter isn't using her fork properly?

"You can't eat like that, Peter".

"Er, sorry, Mrs. Venton?".

"You can't eat like that".

"Umm...".

"Your fork's upturned, like a shovel. That's not the correct way to eat your fried egg. Or beans, come to that".

Not that much different from her daughter. Redoubtable.

"She's right." Grunting Fenella concurs. "It's because he's left-handed. Or stupid".

"Peter. Just look at me. Let me show you. No! Not her! Me!"

"Er... ok".

"You pick up your fork, turn it over. Bring it down my the egg. With your right hand. No! The right hand!" Left-handedness also affected my logical reasoning so (you guessed it) I didn't know my left from my right.

Until I was about twelve. Same with my cousin. She's left-handed too.

"Then gently move the knife towards the fork and, together, pull it towards you. Towards you mouth. Open. And eat. There!"

Kind. Actually very kind. Impatient. And particular. A grown up - well, older - version of her wee yin - no doubt.

Smiles around the table. Fenella too. Though her's was possibly more of a sneer - I could never quite tell.

That's the memory. The memory I grasped at for years, when we (or more particularly my wife) were attempting to teach my little girl table manners. That's the reason why I rarely said anything. I was otherwise engaged. Forty-two years back. Feeling a barking or two. From persons then unknown.

So, what was I doing round there for breakfast? I've rattled the cortex for that too. Think it was because we shared transport with The Ventons.

Fenella was big. Not fat. Not heavy. Just big. With glorious wavy hair. Valkyrie. But Celt. Nearly 5 feet tall, which, when you stop to think about it, is big. Like 10-year-old big.

To be honest I can't remember our first meeting. If I had, it would work something like this:

The girl stood at the top of Forefield Rise, nostrils flaring, imperious, Boudicca before lunch. The boy approached, looking worn, be-

draggled. Forefield was a one-in-three. His mother lagged slightly behind, body straining against the forces of gravity, her normally rosy complexion now puce.

To say Fenella's glare was contemptuous would be, well, a whopping understatement. The boy was spoiling her view. And that would not do.

"*Breakfast?*'"

"*Oh, go on then*"

"*Send your mother home*"

Fenella, to put it simply, was an astounding phenomenon. The Eighth Wonder. She was like she looked. And you did not mess. Whatever age.

She knew her own mind like no one could ever have and she was wild, almost feral.

In love? No. I don't think you could say I was in love with Fenella, ever. She was a little too teutonic in looks, though to be honest the main reason why I wasn't was because I'd probably have been too scared to contemplate that sort of thing.

Kind of looked on me as a necessary nuisance, an impedance, an impediment. Actually I think she rather got into her role, over time, of Minder. After a while I think she rather liked me. Like a pet rat or something.

One day we were horsing around at the top of the drive, not far from the parking spot next to Mrs. Sim's house. Mrs. Sim's Siamese made her usual sharp hissing, followed by that plaintive wail. God, if ever a section in a cartoon reflected nature so perfectly it's that Siamese song in Lady and The Tramp. Except here there was only one. More than enough.

Fenella was playing in the flowerbed directly opposite La Sim's kitchen window.

Me: I, er, don't think you can go in there. Mrs Simm.

Fenella: Mrs. Simm is rubbish. What's this? Hmmm... [picks up tennis ball] Catch!

Of course, I'd never caught anything in my life, so I missed in that typical wimpy-way that the wimpy-boy misses in sixties and seventies films. Strange spider movements. Splaying arms and hands over face. Intense look of fear and embarrassment. That sort of thing. Anyway, the ball thudded against the Triumph Toledo. Thud. Like that. Thud. Big Thud. Enormous Turnip Thuddd. Out Mrs Sim darted. Reptilian.

Mrs Sim: What is going on here?

Fenella: Nothing. Just playing. What *you* doing? [Defiant]

(Oh I wanted to shrink and disappear, with Tinkabel, wherever she was, into the first cluster of Rose petals I could find. But there you were. You could never hide. Not when Fenella was around.)

Mrs. Sim: Well, I... You dreadful girl! Just you wait. I'll tell your mother. I'm sure she'll be appalled. And you [pointing at Peter], you should be ashamed of yourself, hanging around with such a young...[getting breathless] a young... THUG.

Fenella: My mum thinks you're a festering prune.

(Now that comment was good. Really good. Like the Sword of Damocles, suddenly flung over the head of Sim, it rendered her speechless. Speechless and powerless. Almost.)

Mrs Sim: Hideous girl. Get off [catching her breath] my [wheeze] [with all the energy she can muster] property!!!

Maybe Fenella was just another girl who happened to live down the road. Maybe she meant so much more. There was one very significant factor. Remember - I had two sisters. Three years either side, too far away to be allies, too close for comfort.

****

Whereas the relationships with older girls and girls outside of school were either unsatisfactory, mildly complicated or both, inside it was always so simple. Maybe that's why it's difficult to remember the day-to-day hum-and-sway of wee chat and other nonsense.

Though wait. There was a time.

Catherine and Judy were two similar girls. Close friends, for sure, more like sisters in fact.

They were both very earnest girls. Very genuine, I guess. Quite expressive. Not pretty. Just very nice.

Catherine looked like Florence - the Magic Roundabout one. Like she'd always just stepped in from a particularly chilly wind. Mousey hair. Very bright. Brainbox.

Judy was similar looking but blonde. And shorter. Together they were like a couple of china dolls. Or maybe Japanese.

Anyway, we had a pretty civilised relationship, the three of us. Tea for three. Aged four, five, six and seven.

Normally Catherine would start.

"Have you done your homework?"

No, hold on, we didn't have homework then, did we?

"Do you want a strawberry, Judy, Peter?"

"Yes, of course. Where did you get them from?"

"Mum always gives me strawberries."

'I thought she gave you sausages'

Sniggers. Catherine's Dad had a sausage plant.

'Where does the plant grow', we'd ask, of course. 'Your back garden?'

"Who you going to marry?" I said to Catherine. "My Dad," she said. "Your Dad?" "Yup, my Dad. He sells sausages". In fact, her Dad made sausages. Well, not him exactly but the people who worked for him. They were sausages you could find at Sainsburys or at Caters. They were Spears Sausages. I used to think this was wow! That was the best thing. I wanted to marry her Dad. Almost.

"You can't marry your Dad!" "Why not?" she asked. I was beginning to get a little worried. "Because he's your Dad." "Oh". Now she was beginning to get worried. Then she rallied. "Why can't I marry my Dad? He's, um, lovely and he gets me dolls and, um, he's tall and he loves us all. And my Mum." You couldn't really argue with that.

"I'd marry my brother," said Judy. This was getting serious. "Same," I said. "You can't marry your brother". Her brother was almost old enough for her to marry, to be honest. He was eleven years older than her. "Well, er, he plays with me and makes me laugh and gets me, um, Spangles. And he lets me play his guitar." Again, great grounds for betrothal.

"Why don't you marry one of your sisters?" asked Zarah.

It was horror. I'm sure it was horror. I stared at them for about thirty seconds. "Bleeeeeuuuuurghhhh!"

A PTTV PRODUCTION

What's the time, Peter?

Hello again. Here we are in the corridor outside Kindergarten, by the School Clock. What's the time? Well, the little hand's pointing to just before the 11 and the big hand's pointing to the 9.

So it's quarter past 11.

CHAPTER 9

July 1970: 1,2,3, Sing!

I think my sensitivity towards music comes from that time. Definitely.

If you stop to think about it that's probably true with everyone, no? Everyone who's bothered about it, anyway.

Music recalls everything. Taste, smell, sight, sound. Touch.

And so, from the pianola on, music had a habit of grabbing me, heightening me, tossing me around a little.

Funny to say but the first thing I think of is hymns. Hymns at The School.

It was the piano. And the voices. The combination.

Daisies are our silver. Sounds very twee. Buttercups are gold. It's just that piano run - the stepping, pedestrian accompaniment, running behind us, attempting to pick us all up. Always on the beat, never wavering. Incredibly reassuring, undeniably English. And very, very pretty. Irresistible, really.

Oh Jesus I Have Promised. The well-known version's a little like Daisies. We learnt that later. But it's the children's version, the upbeat one that sticks. The jauntiness, the catchiness. It was all there.

Then a little later. Father Hear The Prayer We Offer. It's that repeated phrase, just one tone lower, towards the end. Amazing.

Even Praise The Lord Ye Heavens Adore Him. Yes, Deutschland, Deutschland... that one. Loved it. Teutonic, stately. Gorgeous, really.

And, somehow, one hundred young girls singing in unison, out of tune, formlessly, made it even more heart-rending.

There was an amazing version of Now Thank We All Our God. Not the stately, rather dull version you hear on Songs of Praise. If you've ever happened to have watched Songs of Praise, that is. You have, of course you have. You would just never admit it, would you. Anyway. This version was frenetic, frantic almost. It went all over the place. And the girls loved it. Very syncopated too, a bit tricky. And we nailed it, every time.

Yet another sapping of testosterone.

Then, every so often, there'd be something a little more modern. Like Morning Has Broken. And we'd get down from time to time and sing it wrong. "Praise for the Mor-or-or-ning". Groovy Girls.

Kneeling, mostly kneeling.

Little knees you see. Mostly mine were bare knees. Didn't wear tights. Should have got Mum to buy a pair.

Same with crossed legs. Can't imagine sitting like that these days. Or kneeling. I wonder who it was who first thought that that would be a good way to stay on the floor. Sometimes for 20 minutes or more. Hard floor too.

Mind you, can't remember feeling sore. Maybe I never felt sore. Maybe you don't at that age. Maybe little kids are specially designed to kneel and sit cross-legged. With ease.

And then there was the time we did The Lord's Prayer.

Someone brilliant - must have been Miss McKay - had come up with the wheeze of recording the girls singing.

They'd never done it before.

Not only that. Someone was going to make them into actual records. A whole load, so we'd each be able to take one home and listen to it on the second-hand record player with the arm that stacked and released and looked like a big suitcase.

Wow! Triple wow! Now that was exciting.

And the track all the kids would be grooving to in the disco-theque was...?

The Lord's Prayer.

We seemed to rehearse it for weeks and weeks! Or maybe longer. Maybe we rehearsed it all term.

It was a very simple tune. We could have had it nailed in less than an hour, easily. I think it was just that Miss-mmm wanted perfection and she was damned well going to get it. No sacred stone was left unturned. No syllable and no nuance. So thy kingdom came to whoever deserved it, thy will was done, whether via fantastic presents for Christmas or World War III. It was He who gave us our daily bread, not Mum or Da. They just picked it up from Sainsburys or it came with the milk. So the milkman was an angel, obviously. I'd never trespassed in any case - was far too scared of Mrs. Simm - so there was nothing for God to forgive me. And I can't remember anyone so much as coming to collect a ball or tossing their cabbages over the wall from the allotment, so there was nothing for me to forgive, to anyone, either. Leading us not into temptation was touched upon, though not thoroughly turned over, for some reason. But by the time we were ready to record, there was absolutely no doubt at all that we would all most likely be delivered from evil and that His was the kingdom, no pretenders, not even Marc Bolan. And the power. And the glory. Forever. And ever. So let it be so.

And then The Big Day came. At last.

For some reason I can't remember much paraphernalia, much equipment. Maybe there were a couple of mics at either side of the assembly room. It wasn't a very big room, by the way. It was where 1B had their lessons, where I would be next year. But they still managed to fit one hundred and thirty girls in there without too much of a squeeze. And what must have been at least some recording stuff.

We must have done about ten takes. Ten more times through the thing.

Then it was done.

And a month later, when we'd all forgotten about it...

There it was. Or they were, more to the point. Over one hundred little discs, as shellac-ed as could be (boy, they were solid, thick things). But they were beautiful. I must have played that record time and time again. So that's probably over a hundred times in the space of 6 months. The Lord's Prayer. As sung by Bankton High Junior School, years Kindergarten to 1A. Predictably, it was the record of 1971. Though not, as you can imagine, 1972.

I don't think I ever listened to it again.

****

Miss Moira McKay.

Missummakiye.

God, we loved her. All of us, every one girl of us. She was amazing. Charismatic, enthusiastic, lyrical, lovely. And (and this is the crucial thing) it wasn't really her looks that made her so. It was her love of Music that did it.

For Moira McKay was the Music Teacher. Or the Pied Piperette. Mary Poppins. With a piano.

In retrospect, she was a very Old School Teacher. But then, I suppose, who isn't?

To begin with, there were the Vocal Exercises. Very haughty though appealing, in a haughty kind of way.

"The tip of the tongue, the lips and the tcccccttttth!"

"Me, me, me, me, me, me, me, me, meeeeeee"

"La, la, la, la, la, la, la, la, laaaaaaa"

Then up a tone and so on and so forth. Like clockwork. We liked that. Tuneful familiarity.

Then there'd be a song to learn. Usually from that book with the 50s looking children's choir (actually, it looked more like an orchestra) peering out from the cover.

Then we'd bash a few things. Glockenspiels, drums, wood-blocks, those one-note bar thingies, heads.

Then we'd have a re-cap of a couple of songs we all knew. Favourites? "Riding on a Donkey", "Bobby Shaftoe", "Oh Soldier, Soldier". More I'm sure, though those are the ones to have wafted their way down the years most resonantly.

Music teachers are quite often on to a good thing. Off to a flyer, with kids. All they have to do is sing. Smile. And sing. Kids tend to like that. Now. And then. Miss McKay did this of course but somehow she did more. Most music teachers play a bit role in the life of the school they work in but she could have been running the place for all we knew.

Miss McKay was mesmerising. All us girls fell in line. I think it was her face. She had dark black hair - wavy I think. Must have been late thirties though could have been younger. She had a stern serenity, most of the time but her smile made you feel that she'd like you forever, so long as you just sang the following song correctly.

Because Music to her was as much about correctness as about anything else. You could never allow yourself to think that subjective things like taste had anything to do with it.

She once got us to bring in our favourite musical record. I think we were all six or perhaps seven by then.

I could have picked any of my many bits of pretty vinyl. Or Sarah's or even Mum or Dad's come to think of it. Uncle Mac or The Campdown Races, for example. Or Dickie Henderson sings songs from Cinderella. Or West Side Story. No, that wasn't Dickie, that was Larry Kert and Chita Rivera. Or The Well-Tempered Clavier.

I chose Pinky and Perky. Their version of Cinderella Rockerfeller. With that chap with the low voice who used to sing along, the one who sounded like he had hiccups.

I thought it was rather good.

Missemakiye hit the roof. She was completely and utterly livid. That an intelligent pupil like Peter, with his proven singing AND acting abilities should stoop so downright low. That I should dare to have been so sloppy, lazy and ignorant to have chosen such a piece of crap. If she hadn't have been really the most lovely person in every little girl's world she would have stamped on the thing then and there and thrown it in my face, in front of all my girlmates.

She was so disappointed.

Shame on you, Peter, and never darken my grey lino again with such appalling rubbish.

I seem to remember, much later, having a similar effect on my English teacher when I attempted to extol the many and various virtues of Rod McKuen. But that's another story.

****

Music wasn't all about Missem. There was of course Music Time, the quite fabulous-ly old-fashioned (even then) music programme the Beeb put out weekly to "Schools and Colleges". "1...2...3...SIIIING!" Like a production assistant had shot a 5000 volt thunderbolt through the presenter's bum. I liked the way the two of them sat on either side of the telly screen, as if they were trying to sit as far away from each other as possible.

Not forgetting, of course, the bonus of the 2 minute introduction ident-thingy, at the start of each programme. I think they put that there to hypnotise the kids. That diamond thing that did psychedelic things. And that strangely attractive music. Those are the things you really remember.

Anyway, Miss McKay would remain possibly the most fragrant of all fragrant things at The School for me. And, as you've probably noticed by now, that school was the most fragrant of all schools. And being diverted by fragrancy was perhaps not the best way to begin a education. Or begin anything for that matter.

It was definitely the most pleasurable though.

CHAPTER 10

Preparing to be a domestic goddess

Did I ever long for the week to end?

Like when I was older at Big School?

Or now?

Did I ever get that edgy Sunday feeling? A fear of Monday?

Like later. Or now? Now, when I wish Monday would just disappear into the nine circles of hell whence it came.

No. Never. Don't think I ever did.

Because those years were simply there - they just happened. Just moved on. With a gentle momentum all their own.

And I never felt fear. Nor the pain of middle age, the semi-constant dread of let-down, disappointment and inevitable failure.

Maybe it's true what they say. That comes to everyone at nine, everything else being relatively non-traumatic. Your paranoia, your sensitivities, your pre-pubescence even.

Who knows? All I remember is nothing special. Nothing special about weekends. They just merged with the weeks. Beautifully untouched and simple. Oblivious.

It was only when Nigel came along that I started to feel anything like anxiety. The beginnings of the everyday feelings now. Fear, anxiety, self-pity, aimlessness. All that mortal stuff.

And I just accepted everything.

Apart from anything else, being a girl was a cinch.

****

I remember making lilies.

I was about as good at craft as I was at art. Not so good. But what's interesting is that, like the Tremendously Triffic Totem Pole event that lily making was rather an achievement. And put me in pretty good stead for the rare occasions we had posh dinner parties when I was much older.

I think it must have been what they call a supply teacher these days. Or maybe even a parent. Someone who didn't normally appear in the school. Was she pretty? Was she some kind of Special Guest? I'm really not sure.

She must have been pretty special though. Because, one day, I think in the Summer of 1970, she came to our class and taught us all how to make a paper lily.

Now what's interesting is that this class could safely be called "Domestic Science". Or "How to be a Young Lady". Not that, once again, I minded. I never minded bending gender.

Have you ever made a paper lily? Not such a silly question. Because a paper lily is one of the most perfect craft-y things you could ever make. And it makes those paper napkin things look dead classy, I can tell you. Better that folding them in half (triangle-ways) as if you were laying out tea for your Auntie Aggie. With bad Mr Kipling iced cakes. And weak tea.

No, these lilies make for beautiful accompaniments to the poshest of posh cream teas in Mayfair. Or a high class dinner at The Ivy at somesuch. That good.

Take a paper napkin, unfold it completely, then fold four corners into the middle. Then fold the four corners in again, again into the middle. Make sure you do it carefully so that no spaces are left uncovered, including those edgy bits. Then turn the resultant flat napkins over and do it again, one more time. Now you're ready to do the pulling. Pull the little bits of triangle paper sticking out from between the folded edges, one at a time. Eventually the paper napkin will take on the appearance of a curled-up lily. There you go. I remembered! Again!

All because I followed the instructions of a supply teacher nearly forty-five years ago. She must've been pretty. And special.

It's funny because it's often the simplest of things which are the most perfect. And of course the most memorable. And that's what makes your first school impressions so important. And, possibly, so disarming, so dangerous.

Because perfect things don't last, do they? Particularly when they're created in a perverse environment. One that was almost unreal, that shouldn't have been.

A PTTV PRODUCTION

Going to School

Time for a story. This story's called Fenella and the Peaches.

Once upon a time there was a big girl called Fenella. Well, she was pretty big for her age. She was 6 and was twice as big as her normal friend, Peter.

She and her mum had just done the shopping. The doorbell rang and in came Peter, all huffy and puffy because he had just run up the drive at Butt Ash and all along the road to their house, the nice one with the flat roof.

"Mum's bought peaches. Want one?" said Fenella, looking like Don't Care.

"Yeah. I love peaches," said Peter.

"We'll take the bag with us," she said, pulling Peter by his shirt up the stairs.

"Where we going?" he said. "We normally sit in your kitchen!"

"Not going there today. It's sunny so we're going on the roof," said Fenella.

"But didn't your mum say…?" began Peter.

"She says 'What you don't know can't hurt you'. So that means that she won't know and you won't tell her, stupid," said Fenella.

"Ah. OK. Yeah, alright. Let's go." Peter was scared and excited. He hadn't been on a roof before. It was his adventure for the day so that made him smile inside.

They stood in Fenella's bedroom next to a sort-of-step next to a large window.

"Right. You go first. Go on, I've got to get you up there first, haven't I, Banana Face," said Fenella.

"Ah, oh, alright then. I'm... you will hold on, won't you?" Peter asked. He felt very, very wobbly.

"Scaredy cat! You're only going through an open window. Go on! It's like a door. I just... need... to... push... a little... there! You're out!"

Peter stood there on the roof. It was flat. "Wow!" he thought. "It's not like other roofs. And you really can stand on it."

Then he looked. He had woozy feelings in his tummy. He could see out into the street except that this time he was above the street. Miles above.

Fenella just jumped out. Everything was easy for Fenella. She had the bag of peaches.

"Want another?" Fenella sat down.

"Sit, doggy! Go on, you're not going to fall over the edge. You're miles away. Here it is." Fenella gave Peter the peach.

He ate it and sat there with the peach stone in his hand. Fenella snatched it away.

She then told Peter about what happens when you throw a peach stone away.

"My dad says that if you throw a peach stone away it goes into the ground and becomes a big peach tree," she said, smilingly.

"Like this!" And with that, the peach stone disappeared over the edge of the house.

"Bet it grows as big as the house. Even bigger. Bet it's as big as the beanstalk! Bigger!" Fenella was getting too big for her boots again.

Fenella ate her peach, then gave Peter the stone.

"Go on, you do it now!"

"I don't know, I…" said Peter

"Go on Piddle Pants. True, dare, double-dare, kiss or promise? I double dare you!"

"But isn't it…?" Peter didn't like being naughty.

"Peter's a scaredy piddle pants, Peter's a…" Fenella was always naughty.

Then Peter thought that no one would see so he threw his stone over the edge, just like Fenella.

"There. Easy, wasn't it, poopy knickers!"

"Ow!"

"What was that?" asked Peter.

"What was what?" asked Fenella.

"That noise. Someone said ow!" said Peter.

"Didn't hear anything," said Fenella.

"What the hell was that? For goodness' sake," said someone.

"What…? Who's there? Answer me!" said someone again, angrily.

Peter felt scared. What's more, he thought he knew who that voice belonged to. And it made him feel even more scared.

Fenella started laughing.

"Stop it! They'll hear you!" cried Peter.

Fenella couldn't stop laughing. Then, for no real reason, except that he could feel it rising in his tummy, Peter started laughing too.

They were still rolling around, there on the roof, there at the top of the house when a voice shouted, "Fenella!"

Immediately, Fenella stopped.

Peter kept on laughing his silly socks off. He was having *such* a good time!

Fenella's mum jumped through the window, just like Fenella had and flew down on her like a soaring eagle or a snowy owl when it catches a mouse.

There was some scuffling. Peter thought he heard Fenella grunt. Then came a sort of whooshing in front of him and the next thing Peter knew was that he was sitting on a chair in the Sitting Room.

He felt very red. Fenella was sitting next to him. She looked red too.

And you'll never guess who was sitting there, right in front of the two of them.

Yes, that's right. Mrs. Sim.

"Who threw that stone?", said Mrs. Sim.

"Neither," said Fenella.

"Me," said Peter.

"What are you....?" said Fenella.

"You could have killed me, dreadful boy!" said Mrs. Sim.

"Say sorry, Peter", said Fenella's mum.

"Sorry, Mrs. Sim," said Peter.

"Why did you go on the roof, Fenella? How many times have I told you?" said Fenella's mum.

"Four hundred and fifty one, Mummy," said Fenella.

"Go to bed immediately! No tea for you, young lady!" said Fenella's mum.

"Don't care!" said Fenella. And with that, she stood up and went upstairs, struffily.

"You need to keep that daughter of yours under a tight leash, Portia," said Mrs. Sim. "She's a disgrace. She's rude and disrespectful. I'd have given her a good hiding. That'd have sorted her out. My children would have never done that!"

"How are James and Marion, Gladys? Must be a while since you've seen them. Six years, is it?" said Fenella's Mum.

Peter bent down to pick up a biscuit up off the plate beside him and when he looked up, Mrs. Sim had completely disappeared.

Just like the shopkeeper in Mr. Benn.

And that is the story of Fenella and The Peaches.

CHAPTER 11

Specs and other embarrassments

Why specs? Why me? Why at 5?

You're up there, high on the crest of a wave - girls at your beck and call, teachers receptive to your ever-expanding intellect. Riding the Rainbow Books like a Wild Swan. Adding, subtracting - all a doddle.

Then it comes. Your first major setback.

And you barely notice it. But it's the thing that, if I'm honest, set me back a long way. Long way back.

When I was 3 I got measles. Barely noticed them. I remember I had them at the same time (I think) as Sarah and there was an afternoon when we were both lying on the sofa at home. That was it. Measles, The Illness.

So I had measles. No big deal.

Except that, when I was five and a half I got fitted for glasses. I can't even remember why. Certainly can't remember not seeing much. All I remember is that it was made into an exciting time by Mum (and possibly Da, can't remember). Glasses - brilliant. You can pick your own style and everything. Look. Green horn-rimmed. Or maybe they were transparent brown. Beige. Put them on. You look lovely.

So I got psychologically dealt with. Damage limitation. Voila. Specs. On my face. I remember a disconcerting feeling. Just once. The first day I wore them at The School. No fanfares, no "ooh, you look great, Peter". Just Ugly. Ugly Peter. Fleetingly Ugly Peter. For the first time. It wasn't a shock or anything. Just a small bit of disconcertment.

That disconcerting feeling would come and go. But it was

there now. You couldn't get rid of it. Plastic horn rims and lenses. Milk bottles. My eyesight was quite bad. I hadn't even noticed. Measles. Something I hadn't suffered with at the time. Now I was being made to suffer. Delayed, displaced reaction, suffering. Disconcertment. Forever.

Don't think the girls or the teachers ever looked at me with the same admiring gaze again.

Then again. Maybe my eyes had been so bad that I hadn't properly seen their true reaction to me in the first place! Maybe it wasn't admiration after all.

****

Shorts. Thinking about it now, why shorts?

Why long, itchy socks?

Why shorts? They kept your knees bare, which meant of course lots of flesh wounds, particularly in the early School days, particularly on that tarmacky stuff.

Looked pretty silly. Though possibly cute. But silly. And impractical, certainly. I guess proof is in the simple fact that noone of that age wears shorts anymore. Longs are the thing now, aren't they? OK, so granted, if you live in New South Wales your little mate is going to wear shorts and a polo shirt but in those days it was...

1 cap, green and grey with school emblem on the front.

1 white shirt, polyester - as now - long sleeves for winter, short sleeves for summer. I may have made that bit up.

Shorts.

Long grey socks which folded over your knees but which did not stop grazing.

And then... you wore shorts. Grey shorts, which came to just above the knee, whatever height - 3 feet 2 inches, 3'6", 4'2", 4'6".

Shorts and a cap. Oh God.

****

Frequently I reflect on why. Why the hell I was sent there. It was beautiful, probably, for at least a year. Possibly the most beautiful year of my life. It's just it puts the rest in a peculiar place. Boys school. The Sensual World. The Sexual World. Relationships with family - Dad, Sisters, even Mum. Life partnership. Then full circle. To beautiful offspring. Just as well he's a girl then.

CHAPTER 12

Summer 1970: A Thoroughly Decent Summer Holiday

Sublime. Most likely. No, most definitely. The first year was sublime. A haze of parties, lemon balm, poster paints, smiles, cocktail sausages, Mary, Rosemary, Judy, Mungo, Sarah, Midge, Zarah, Jane. Fenella. And others.

Then Summer. And a girl called Tracey.

Tracey from East London. On a Goodly Deed Scheme.

There was a lot of that in those days. In more subtle ways there probably still is. People born with nothing to worry about materially, brought up to aspire to something, to tell good from bad, shielded from the horrors of adulthood, or maybe just the adulthood of adulthood. Who think it'd be good to take care of, from time to time and without too much sacrifice, little people worse off than themselves and their little ones. Missionary zeal, you could call it.

Anyway, Mum had that stuff in droves. And she felt, at the beginning of the seventies, that it would be *very good* if we had one of these people to feel better about.

Tracey came from what I'd been told was a broken home. "Broken" brought instant thoughts of broken windows, upturned furniture, cracks in the telly. It's a funny expression. I seem to remember her family consisted of a load of elder brothers, a Dad who was rarely around and possibly no mother at all. That could be wrong - Mum could have extended her zeal to fantasy - but that's how they often came in those days. Here was someone with not much, essentially. And we were all doing her a favour, a change as good as a rest and all that.

Fact was, she was lovely. But older, like so many others. So there was no way I was going to have a little boy's crush on her. Just admiration from afar, as per. Most of the time she spent with Sarah anyway. Like they did. But that's another story.

She had this amazing accent.

We didn't have accents, fairly obviously, not us nice Kays. Well, Mum had had a fairly broad Lanacastrian accent but you didn't really notice it anymore, except if you were on the phone to her, then of course it unmasked her. No, the only accents I really knew then belonged to Misses Huxtable and White, the cleaners. The accent in Bath, the working class, non-excessively-posh-received-daaarrrling-kind-of-accent sounded a little what you might call harsh-ooaarrr. That's to say, not as pleasant as the ones you got down the road in Midsomer Norton, Frome or Shepton Mallett. These were urban, slightly spat-out accents. At least those spoken by the younger owners. Actually Misses Huxtable's and White's accents were ok.

But Tracey's accent was amazing. Like the people off The Good Old Days. Almost like Dick Van Dyke's. Strident, affirming, no-one-messes-with-me accent.

And I'm sure Mum (and possibly Dad) was a little nervous about how well behaved or otherwise she might be.

She turned out to be brilliant. As communicative and co-operative as any seven year-old I've ever known, then or (most definitely) now.

And she had a very serene smile. Like her mind had created her own world of beauty, which she was more than content with for now, right up until the real one came along.

There's a photograph. It still exists. Rainbow Woods, August 1970, I think. In the clearing. Up on Coombe Down. Just me and the Little Girl, doing a plie or somesuch. Not that she knew that. And me, standing there, the Little Lemon, with my hands down by my tummy, grinning at the camera. We're both grinning.

It's possibly the most perfect photograph in the World.

Then we had a great holiday in Cornwall.

Whatever happened to roof racks? You don't see them much, if at all, anymore. Which is stupid, if you ask me. It's an essential part of British culture, Dads struggling with the buggers the night before take off.

We'd always be last minute. Always. And Dad would always be Buggering and Shitting more than usual as a result. My bag was probably last to leave the house. Or maybe I had more help than I remember and Mum did it all. Whatever, Dad would still be at it at eleven o'clock or so, pulling the octopus leads as tight as they would go over the ancient, massive, excessively heavy, suitcases. The ones Mum had dusted down after Dad had heaved them down (more Buggering and Shitting) from the loft.

We'd normally get up very early indeed to go anywhere on holiday. That's because, back then, you'd be hard pushed to find any motorway to get you to where you wanted to go. We might have had the M4, which took us to near Reading but that wasn't much use to us. And the M6 went up to where Mum used to live and we had already been up there but that was the Lake District, that wasn't Cornwall.

The M5 was many years off and Dad had worked out that it would take us over 8 hours to get to Helston, which is where we were off.

So we set off at 8 in the morning. By my reckoning asked whether we were there yet twenty times before we eventually arrived!

There was definitely a complex and uniquely British Family Car Culture in those days. Maybe because most holiday journeys took so long and there weren't as many diversions, culinary or otherwise, en route.

Sandwiches were always packed. These were normally a selection of egg sandwiches (not the most practical thing), scotch eggs, Penguin or Club biscuits and flasks of orange squash.

On the way there...

Sarah would always take the window seat as she was the most vocal prima donna in the party. For the most part, I'd be in the middle, though I think was relegated to this space more often than I give her credit.

There would always be waving. I don't see much waving these days at all, possibly because people are far more chary of nasty things like road rage but in the early seventies waving was a national kiddy pastime. A necessity. We'd do it as much as possible. It was brilliant fun and, for the most part, you'd get the driver behind to wave back. I think.

A child would nearly always be sick. Sarah first, then me, then . I think this was the era of Sarah mostly but me fairly frequently. was still too small to be sick, though suffered later much more than us, possibly because her memory of car journeys between the ages of, say, 2 and 10, was more horrifically vivid than ours.

There would always be games. Mostly "I-Spy" or "Animal, Vegetable or Mineral a.k.a. Twenty Questions", based on the popular radio show which we all loved. I think I came up with the American Director Raoul Walsh once - "Don't you mean Raquel Welch?" - which almost caused World War III in the back.

We'd always get lost. I'm sure nearly every family who ever went on holiday in a car did.

And Dad would always end up in a long queue. Then he'd get stressed. Very stressed. Grinding teeth, strange growling, whining even. More "come ons" than were necessary. Possibly 100 more.

More pressure on the old heart.

We'd get there in the end of course, wherever we were going. And, exactly like most of the holidays I can remember, we'd pass a milestone of sorts, a memorable sight, not three miles from our destination. This time it was the gurt telescopes on Goonhilly Downs. Jaw-dropping for a five year-old.

Dad had been pretty accurate. Almost exactly 8 1/2 hours after we had left, we arrived, a little crumpled, at a B&B near Helston, Cornwall.

I think this was possibly the end of the golden days of holidays in-land. British holidays. Compulsory bucket and spade. Later in the 70s Spain (mostly) came calling for most (though we never got that far - France was more our bag, as it tended to be for relatively impoverished middle-class types).

But Cornwall in those days had everything to keep the folks on Blighty Firma. Particularly for kids under seven.

It's that feeling, normally on the 2nd day. You know the one. That one you'd been waiting all summer for? Maybe all year? Driving over the rolling greeny-brown fields, then down through a rickety village with pretty stone cottages, one or two thatched, perhaps with blue doors, round a corner, the beginning of a very steep hill and then...

The crescent of hill and trees, clear blue skies above and, in the middle, sea! There really was no other feeling like it. Why? Who knows? Who cares, really. Maybe it's the first experience us Middle Englanders got of escape. Freedom.

All I know for certain is that it felt flipping brilliant.

Once Da had driven us to the inevitable massive car park, with an inevitable 15 minute walk to our destination, there'd be no shortage of sun, sea and sand. No shortage of buckets and spades, all different colours. And no shortage of people. Hordes of them. I was never aware that any of us seemed to mind about that - surprising looking back, particularly when it came to Dad. I think I rather liked crowds - made it seem really exciting to me, as if it were somewhere you were supposed to be. Where everyone went.

Conventional little bloke I was.

Another brilliant thing about holidays in those days, particularly this one, is that cousin Gerrie would always come and visit. As she lived in Exeter she was just round the corner (well, 2 hours away, anyway). This gave us welcome respite from, well, each other really.

Gerrie was 23, recently qualified as a teacher and the most totally typical older cousin-type you could ever imagine. For a start, she was at the time sort of gender-less. Or perhaps gender-neutral as they'd say these days or non-binary. A they, not a she. But that was then so to us, "she" was a didn't-really-notice-or-care-that-she-was-gender-less brilliant person who could always be relied upon to turn up at exactly the right moment to carry out cousin-ly duties. Like help with the washing up. Or chat with us about school or stuff on the telly or why we probably shouldn't think bad of our brother or sister. Or drive us hilariously badly to a party.

I could relate a book-load of other stories about tussles with roundabouts, upside-down moments in ditches (she drove a VW Beatle) or driving the wrong way down the motorway. Her mum was just as bad. Auntie Jelly lived in Paris. On one infamous UK family visit, whilst driving (if that's the right word) her hire car, she continuously attempted to change gear by winding down her window. I don't she ever got out of first the whole time she was here!

Anyway, Gerrie came in the second week, just after Mum and Da had hurrumphed themselves away from the first B&B, early as it turned out, as they weren't too keen on the landlady. Can't remember why - she must have done dodgy eggs or something. Anyway, I seem to remember we stayed on a farm in the second week, like most people did in those days (more so, probably, than in B&Bs). It smelled not of pig shit but of cider, as I recall. Think I might even have had some, well, a taste anyway. Of cider, that is.

So - after 2 weeks of sea, sand and suntan, we tootled back.

And the car, as usual, would break down.

Cars tended to do that a lot in those days. Ours did, anyway.

So an eight-and-a-half hour journey would be extended by... oh - doubled, at least.

No one really seemed to mind.

Or maybe that's my memory playing tricks on me again.

CHAPTER 13

Another Boy

So, after the timewarp that was Summer, came...

Transition.

After Kindergarten came Transition. Why Transition? These days it's so much more straightforward. Nursery, Reception, Year 1 and so on. Then it was Kindergarten and Transition, with 1B and 1A to come. Pretentious? Possibly. Complicated? Well of course.

Same again? Same as Kindergarten? Another year of sublime shielding from the Real World? Hedges, Banks, that smell and the view?

Not quite. It was all looking so promising. A different class-room, a nice new teacher. Girls pleased to see me after the break.

But Nigel.

Nigel looked like Paul McCartney. Of course he did. And he was the second boy that the girls had to look after. And they were getting a little used to me (particularly since the onset of Specs) so they could do with a bit of spice. A little boy who looked like Paul McCartney would do very nicely thank you.

What's more. Nigel's folks were rich. Nice. Very nice in fact. But rich. Very rich. They lived in Batheaston in an elongated modern Big House (not exactly Mansion but it was Big enough). There were four of them. Nigel's sister Dawn, his Mum and Dad. Think they were called Eleanor and David. Though it might have been Peter. Or even John. No, it was Roy. Definitely Roy. Anyway, John or Peter or David or Roy had made a lot of money out of beds. That was the thing in Bath. You were either new money (like these) or an accountant. Or Naval type. There were some advertising types but not many. Johnpeterdavidroy Mr. Benton might have been Nouveau (Mum again) but he was really very pleasant. Very friendly and quite a laugh. And Eleanor was very kind. The thing was...

Nigel was what Mum called "Spoilt". And Spoilt meant the following

1. You had whatever you wanted. This included the Joe90mobile, Battling Tops and loads of PlayDough. More toys later.
2. You ate very little and were very fussy with food. And asked for more and never ate it. That said, you liked liver, which was plain weird.
3. Girls liked you. A lot. Because you didn't care.
4. You were occasionally (but not always) very mean.
5. You were Thick.

Spoilt did however have its plus points. This meant the following

1. I got to play with the toys. And even borrowed the Joe90mobile.
2. I got to feel smug about the fact that I ate everything. And more. Even though I was a stick. Which made Mum (and Dad possibly) feel good about me. Mr. and Mrs. Harper were of course suitably impressed.
3. Girls still liked me. They just liked Nigel better, that's all.
4. There was nothing beneficial about 4.
5. I was not thick. And got to show it.

Oh. One more thing. For now. Nigel's family were so rich they had a Colourtelly. This Colourtelly was housed, yes housed, in a massive great cabinet. With doors and everything. And when you switched it on it was Colour. Well, not so much colour actually. It was Green. I remember watching Tom Brown's Schooldays on it. There was a part, The Paper Chase Bit I think, when the boys were running across the top of this grassy knoll and you couldn't make them out at all. Everything had gone green.

I was still impressed though. And felt completely second rate as a result. Nigel had everything and I didn't. And that wasn't good.

Kids are always sharing things. When they feel like it, that is.

I can't remember sharing that many things, despite the fact I was born on a Friday. Love Hearts, of course, though at 6, strangely, that didn't seem to mean much. Love Bug. Cuddle Me. Gee Whizz. Gee Whizz? All in that semi-invisible writing, barely embossed onto that strange chalky-sherbet-y round sweet.

"D'you want a Love Heart?"

"Yeah"

"Shut your eyes"

"OK"

"Open them again"

"Oh"

"Be Mine"

Would have been nice.

No, maybe it did actually happen. One of the things about being six and slightly stupid is that you tended to miss things. The assumption was that I was an adopted girl - popular enough but by dint of having exchanged my disruptive, destructive boy thing for something more sensitive - something which involved the high-fallutin'. In-depth discussions about Tintin. Or Marine Boy. Or working out who was funnier - Fleagle or Snorky. Rather than trying to kick the hell out of a plastic ball (which was lighter than it should have been anyway) or seeing who was the fastest, had the best shoes or the biggest Matchbox car port.

There were a few girls. Judy was one. She was sweet. Don't think bad of me. Sweet. Rather than cute. Or viciously attractive. Sweet. You could always have a chat. About the stuff above. Or how her Dad was. Or my Mum. Or what it was like to be a vicar's daughter. Think she was a vicar's daughter, anyway. Either that, or he worked for Bath Uni as a lecturer. No, vicar, I'm sure it was. Something earnest, anyway.

"D'you want a Love Heart"

"Of course"

And Debbie? Looked rather German, as I recall. Quite heavy. Nice though.

They were all nice, really.

Zarah. Now she was cute. Though, to be honest, not exactly that cute. She had the sort of looks that could have her mistaken for a little boy - a pretty one at that, but a pretty boy. She was quite short too. Looked younger, somehow.

Funny how time perverts things. When I was seventeen I remember being told about what had happened to Zarah, by Judy. Zarah had turned into something far more exotic, by all accounts. A young-man-eating-young-female. Maybe I was turned on by the rah-rah-taffeta-ness of it all. The poshness of young fuckers. I never met up with her, but the eroticism of it all diverted me entirely from the memory of the real Zarah, the unassuming young boy-girl I'd know at school.

By this time the two girls had both long flown the coop and were boarding at some boys school or other. Because that's what tended to happened. A handful of little boys went to primary girls schools, the fee paying ones. A handful of sixth-form intake, as they say, at fee paying boys schools were, yes, girls. So some of the girls I knew ended up going to boys schools. For two years, not three, granted, but there was a strangely perfect irony to it all. And it was just as messed up too.

Though maybe a little more messed up in fact. Maybe I wasn't that hard done to, after all. Maybe things were more honest then. So I had the pick of the girls - their undivided, loyal, sometimes devoted attention. Pure thoughts included - no ulterior motives, no strangely hormonally erratic behaviour. It's just that I didn't notice it. Because that's the biggest irony of all. Of course you don't notice it. That's because you're five, six. Not fifteen, sixteen. Or fifty.

But when Nigel came along, it all changed. And although you can say that it all changed because of him, you can't say it was his fault, necessarily. He just happened to look like Paul McCartney. He didn't make himself look like that! Even his cockiness wasn't his fault. He got whatever he wanted, whenever. So when he saw a girl he liked, he just helped himself. Didn't want to be looked after, just wanted to be adored.

Victoria adored him. She was a pretty girl with curly blonde hair who joined the girl gaggle at the same time as Nigel, in Transition. And, as such, only had eyes for him. Which queered my pitch a little of course. I was so used to universal respect, admiration, sympathy from nearly all that a ready-made Nigel acolyte brought out the peevish in me.

"You got your conkers?"

"Why?"

"You wanna play?"

"OK"

"You baked them?"

"Yes I baked them"

"Awwwww"

"You put vinegar on yours!"

"That makes it equal. So?!"

"Hello Nigel"

"Hello Victoria"

"I've got 5 new Ladybird books. Want to see?"

"OK"

"But Nigel, you said..."

"Going to see Victoria's books. Bye"

"Humph"

Relationships can be strong at that age. Nigel's and mine became strong, for sure, but like the rivals we were it could be very edgy. And when he was on home turf he could be intolerable.

Most of all, of course, my Idyll Epoch was over. The "Girls and Poor Me Period".

Done.

Dusted.

Gone.

CHAPTER 14

The early 1970s were very interesting. No, they really were. What pisses me off nowadays is that most of the people who bang on about weren't even there.

But I was. So I can tell you that it was interesting. Particularly in Bath. Particularly the people.

And particularly the teachers at The Girls School.

From the top. Or maybe that should be the bottom. The bottom of the school. Kindergarten. And...

There's Miss Ponting. As I recall a "bun woman". Or maybe short and wavy. No, there was something about her upright nature. She was definitely a bun woman. Occasionally. Dark hair. Slim. Attractive but not so much that you'd notice if you were 5.

Or maybe she was.

Memory does that to you. You feel like someone has to be like someone else. Then you recall they probably weren't who they were after all.

Not prim. I don't think I ever saw her in a suit. She wore wavy blouses and modest skirts - pleats probably. Navies and whites. Perhaps a scarf? A few, most likely.

Miss Ponting was straight. As straight as a die. If you did it right, she'd praise you. If not, she'd be very strict. I seemed to be in her good books for the most part. Except, that is, when I got "boisterous".

Yes, boisterous. It's a funny thing to be accused of. Particularly when you're a boy. I sometimes think that I was expected to be a girl. As in, "Now you're in our house, you'll abide by Girls' Etiquette. That means behaving like a nice young lady".

So Miss Ponting got a little stroppy when I was being boisterous. Bit strict. Bit shouty.

And she did like a good smack. Or is that a slap? Smacked legs. Slapped legs?

Slapped legs sounds better, doesn't it. Because I reckon, Miss Ponting was a bit of a sadist on the quiet.

She used to creep up on you. Quietly like. Once, I was larking about, like you do when you're 5 or 6 and boisterous. And a boy. I must have been saying, rather enthusiastically, "I know what it is. The answer. I know. I know." Or something like that. Liked to think I was right from time to time. And liked to show it. Anyway. I was getting a little bit rowdy. Over-enthusiastic, perhaps. Shouting a little, probably. Suddenly, from absolutely nowhere, came this searing pain, somewhere between the back of my thigh and lower part of my calf. Left calf it was. Owwwwwww! And Oooooooh! Really, that bad. Like being hit by a very leathery leather strap. Except this was a hand. Quite a young (and therefore fleshy) hand. About a 29 year-old hand, I'd say.

"KEEP the noise down, Peter".

It wasn't the first time, either. Always on the legs or leg. Never the hand or arm or head. Heads were a favourite with other teachers (though, for the life of me I can't recall any of the other teachers ever laying a hand on my head - maybe that's a man-teacher thing).

She'd do it to the girls of course. I'm not suggesting anything. In any case, in those days, smacking was par for the course. Caning was still used at a lot of schools, so hands and legs was relatively mild.

To me, though, smacking must have meant something fairly serious. There's that feeling, even now. That feeling of shame.

That feeling that the punishment really did fit the crime. In other words, I must have been behaving badly to be hit quite that hard. And for that reason I think it might have worked, the deterrent that is. I certainly didn't get hit very often, not at that school. And only by Mrs Ponting.

In fact, we never really used to think anything of it. It wasn't shocking at all. It was part of life. You would take a whack, you'd stop doing what you were doing that was naughty or disruptive or otherwise anti-social. And that was that. Very sharp, effective deterrent. I'm really not sure what changed things. It was wrong, of course. Well, I think it was. But, come to think of it, if you asked my peer group nowadays whether they thought it was a bad thing, I doubt you'd get anything much more than a muted response. Because it didn't actually harm. Strange that. Very strange.

And, yes, Miss Ponting definitely enjoyed it.

It is strange though. Strange that I remember most vividly what Miss Ponting did to me. The slapping, the strictness and all that. Because she also was at the helm of some pretty fab teaching.

Those Rainbow books were great and I ate them for breakfast, tea and dinner but I wouldn't have got so utterly nourished if it hadn't been for Miss Ponting's nurturing guidance. Not to mention her teaching maths and early science and all that other good stuff.

It's only with adult hindsight that I can appreciate that. Because for years she was the "strict slapper". And I was her unsuspecting and overly excitable victim.

And although I idolised Miss McKay, I'm sure I would have appreciated music just as much without her as with her. So maybe it was Miss Ponting who had more of a real, long-lasting or at least more significant influence that Miss Mmmm.

It's funny how we treat our own history. Maybe that's like all history, who knows?

So, in Transition, there was Mrs. Thompson. Definitely Missis. No nonsense. Kind. Young. Again. Rather neat. Small handwriting. Quite uneventful, actually. She liked me. I liked her. All the girls did. No adoration. Just liked. We'd probably say she was very "responsible" and "professional" now. Decent, at the very least.

In every other respect I really can't remember her.

Or maybe I can. She looked like Lulu. No bad thing. I had a massive crush on Lulu. She was our size for one. Cute rather than vivacious or larger than life, which would have been too much for a wee yin like me. Too much woman, for sure. All these TV people smiled incessantly of course but Lulu's smile seemed genuine, caring almost.

And she wore slightly sexy clothes too.

So, yes, Mrs. Thompson was like Lulu. And, rather like Miss Ponting, hers was a subtle influence.

I never liked Art much, as a subject. It didn't have the same sense of purpose as other subjects. I was always in so much of a hurry, to finish books first or to get the sums done. Art wasn't the same kind of thing at all. You had to take your time, be considerate with your pencils, brushes and paints. And I was just messy. Messy, sloppy Peter.

So Art was the only subject Nigel was better than me at. Probably.

Thanks to Mrs. Thompson, though, and in partnership with Nigel, I did manage to land an artistic coup. A fabulous work of art, in fact. Bold and expressive and most definitely my one and only masterpiece.

In February 1971 Nigel and I were asked to build a totem pole.

I'm sure that thing was ten feet tall. At least. Massive. We must have needed a crane to build and then paint the thing. And a large supersonic van, like the Mystery Machine in Scooby Doo with groovy stripes and everything, except bigger, to take the thing to its place of show.

Actually it was about five feet tall. And someone probably carried it down the hill. Or maybe put it on the back seat of their Mini.

In any case, the wonderful artefact was soon to be put on show at a special Bath Schools Art Show, displaying kids' paintings, sculptures, almost uncategorisable happenings like ours. It was like Vision On but live and without the groovy music.

And - and this was the big deal - our Tremendously Toppermost Totem was going to be in the paper, The Bath Evening Chronicle.

Like the Lord's Prayer Recording, this was a Big Project.

The structure was cardboard boxes, bound together with sellotape, glue, string, ribbon, plasticine, clay, anything sticky we could get our mits on. Think we must have put jam on there at some point. That took us about two weeks. At least. No, actually, it took us two weeks for the first version, which fell apart after about a day or so. The second version took about a week but that fell apart too. Must have been the clay, which crumbled, obviously. In the end Mrs. Thompson stepped in on version three and saved the project in one fell swoop. She was good at that. No nonsense - saving the day where it counted.

Next - this after six weeks, was the painting.

Ask any adult if you mix all the colours in the rainbow what you get and they will reply "white". And that's of course, right. If you're not under ten, that is. Their answer will always be "ginger". Or "biscuit". Or "ginger biscuit". Or "bleeeurgh". The thing is, they're always going to try and make a new colour, something amazing, something new. Because anyone who's six with a paintbrush in their hand is a visionary. A Van Gogh at heart. And they can do magic. Create seminal objets d'art, revolutionary new palettes. Just like our trigantic teetering totem pole and its "it's not ginger, it's a light jerNigel" hue.

We worked forever on that colour. Always trying to make it whatever we thought were the right colour. I don't think we ever really knew what we were going for. I think I was going for black, which was of course the wrong way. Nigel might have been going for an original shade of puce, though I never bothered to ask, specifically.

I think our totem pole had totempol-esque patterns on it. Zig-zags, embossed on using papier mache or somesuch. And a face. I think we fashioned a nose out of a paper cup. Or the corner of a cardboard box. Yes it was the box, definitely. The eyes had bushy eyebrows but that's because I think the paintbrush lost its brush just above the right eye. So we just cut the end of another brush and put it above the left eye. Nice. Tonynewley Totem.

So, after many an afternoon giggling and splattering far more art material over each other than our work, after more zig-zags and noses than was decent, after many, many exasperated groans from Mrs. T, the Splendiferous was done. Finished. And how it towered majestically over all who surveyed it - those under four feet six inches anyway. Once installed at the Bath Schools Art Show, it settled into the annals of Western (England) Culture like the great big Love Totem it was.

Then, in 1B. Miss Higgins.

Now Miss Higgins. There was a woman to remember.

Ronnie Barker. That's all I can think of. Ronnie Barker.

Miss Higgins was a caricature of Miss Higgins. Like a cartoon Miss Higgins. Ronnie Barker doing Miss Higgins. Or someone like her. Judy, I think was her first name.

Quite kind but very stern. Thought like a man. Acted like a man. Looked like a man. In drag. Doing Miss Higgins. Ronnie Barker.

I imagine her now, having a sneaky ciggie with Doreen Norris, Headmistress and Doris to most who knew her, in the Common Room. Bone china. A cup of Oooo.

Like sisters. Or Spinsters of this Parish. Doris and Judy.

"Gingham. We should have stuck with Gingham, Doris"

"Oh no. D'you see floral is *much* more becoming. D'you see?"

"I do see but... I disagree."

"Disagree? Juicy I think gingham is very old and rather passé. Floral is so much more now. The parents will all approve, I'm sure. Not to mention the little darlings. Juicy?"

"But it's a uniform. Oh Doris, you're a slave to fashion"

"And you, Judy, Juicy, are very Old Hat"

Miss McKay was 1A. I didn't have her as form mistress. Sarah did.

So I had Miss McKay as a girl's teacher before my elder sister did.

Now there aren't many boys who can say that!

CHAPTER 15

Living in a box

The duvet-wrapped life of a girl's school affected my home life too. If I'd have been at a primary or single-sex boys prep or some such there would no doubt have been weekend activities - football matches - played or spectated - swimming, ditto. Instead, my life was full of just one thing.

Telly.

I loved telly. I lived telly. Telly was how I understood the world, how I built ideas, how I found myself. The sixties had revolted apparently and Telly was there, at the centre of it all. And there was I, being spat out at the end of it, revelling in it, digging it like the little wet sponge I was.

We rented a telly. Yes, rented it. Disposable goods cost so much more in those days. You had to be quite well off to own a telly. So a lot of people rented them. You could go Radio Rentals. They were the big one.

But we went Telefusion. The curious thing about these companies is that they seemed to control the transmission of the local signal. Or something. Something like that was what I was told. So that, occasionally - actually frequently - the telly would go snowy. And we'd have to ring the local Telefusion transmission station and ask them when normal service would be resumed. "We don't know. Our engineers are working on it". Normally it would be out for 2 hours, sometimes much longer. I guess it made it all more DIY, more

You'd get a telly with one of those circular dials. Black & White of course. Those push button things on the new sets you actually bought (if you were Croesus-rich as Da would say) were a little space-age. We had a dial. Or maybe three dials. One day

I'll find out and we'll be reunited, Telly and Me. Anyway, you turned the dial and different channels would come on. If you owned a telly or went Radio Rentals you only had three channels. BBC1, BBC2 and ITV. ITV was Harlech Television, later HTV. And that was rubbish. All the commercial TV stations were split into regions. And, if you were the Somerset, Gloucestershire and Wiltshire regions, you got HTV. Which was one of the smaller, poorer stations, so it got all the networked TV but very little foreign stuff because they couldn't afford it.

But our telly was with Telefusion. So we got not 3, not even 4, but 5 TV stations. If you were adventurous and you kept turning the dial you could pick up Westward TV. Another relatively impoverished station but the opening sequence was fantastic. All pastoral and gorgeous with sea-shanty folky coastal music. And they had some Australian shows. Like Skippy. Loved Skippy. Morning, Skip. And the quite inspired continuity-bunny, Gus Honeybun.

"Here's another lovely card. And (pauses to turn the card the right way up) this one's from Emma in Dartmouth. And Emma's going to be 3 today. Happy Birthday, Emma. And Emma would like 3 bunny hops." Gus bounces 3 times.

"And this card's from Peter. And Peter's going to be 6 tomorrow. And (squints) Peter would like Gus to turn out the lights. Very well then, Gus. You know what to do."

Actually that last one never happened. Peter, that is. But for everyone else, Gus'd do a head stand, turn out the lights, bounce up and down, wink. Everything. Loudly. Those studios were very cramped so you'd hear the puppeteer thrashing around, bumping into all sorts of exotic TV ephemera.

Keep turning that dial and you were into totally unknown territory. And you were in for a treat. Station No. 5 was very special. Bit grainy - the main transmitters were miles away. But I did manage to pick up ATV. The Midlands Station. And ATV, of course, was the Big One. Part of Lew Grade's empire. You'd think I wouldn't know that kind of thing when I was 5, 6 or 7 but I did. Strangely precocious little girl I was at times.

Anyway, ATV was splendiferous. They had everything. That wonderful woodcutter who used to show fabulous cartoons and clips of the wild outdoors (American). One day I'll find out what that was called. Then there was a beautiful Australian cartoon series about the groovy animals who lived in a house together. To (later) The Protectors and The Persuaders and The Baron, Randall and Hopkirk Deceased. All that good stuff. And all during the day. HTV would never show that stuff, so noone I knew ever saw it. But I could get it any time I liked.

Of course, I watched the BBC stuff too. But that was later in the day. Normally. Jackanory. Though that was usually holding fare for the main event and just to see how long 15 minutes felt like. Which was, of course, a very long time. Then there'd usually be some kind of drama thing. There was one involving kids at a school with quite a groovy title, which evades me. And Blue Peter of course. Stalwart. Well, not quite. The beautiful thing about the Beeb in the sixties and the seventies is that it didn't patronise. It didn't really know how to. In hindsight, those early TV presenters were probably like rabbits in the headlights. And because of that they came over as fresh, non-formulaic and utterly, fantastically, Britsh-ly eccentric. It was comfortable, cosy, yes but it was always original and that made it compelling. And the enthusiasm and, often, genuine wonder of, in particular, John's explorations into his own derring dos was more than palpable. It was actually fantastic. There was energy, passion in those voice-overs. And the content was always compelling. It was proper magazine stuff, real education - informative, fun and exciting. And I wasn't very groovy so I didn't quite get Magpie, which seemed less reassuring and a bit formless. And Susan Stranks wasn't quite my thing. But that was because I was a nice girl.

I liked some programmes, not so much because of the content but because of the way they were dressed up. Animal Magic was one of those. Of course, like a lot of kids programmes at the time, the presenter was reassuringly familiar. You just liked watching and listening to him. You liked his conversational animalese. Who didn't? But, for the most part, I wasn't that struck on stuff about animals. No, what I liked most about Animal Magic was its closing sequence. God that signature tune was fantastic - the ending in particular. How did they know kids would like that?! It was about a hundred years old then! Well it wasn't but it sounded like it. It wasn't just the tune that got me. I think whoever was in charge of that sort of thing had designed a machine that made the studio disappear and be replaced by using a circular vignette thing. Then you'd have this collage of animals doing animal stuff on a black background until the great big latin bongo hoopla, having done its repeat-y ending bit, finally finished it off with a beautiful upwards glissando followed by the big full stop drum - "Do-wee! Bom". Now that was an ending to end all endings.

I'll bet my gravestone that you can't find that ending anywhere in the world now. Apparently Auntie's got rid of most of the 454 episodes, starting with the oldest first. They were the best ones! God she can be a silly thoughtless bitch sometimes!

Friday, obviously, at five-to-five. Was Crackerjack. It's amazing how you can turn a really simple thing, like a pencil, into a much sought-after treasure. Of course the actual big prizes they won at the end were incredibly exotic. Like Etch-a-Sketch. But the Crackerjack pencil, like the Blue Peter badge (even more sought-after and prized) now that was the thing. I wonder if anyone actually still owns one.

And then there were always those five-minute postscripts to the main batch of kids' programmes. Like Magic Roundabout. Or Sir Prancelot. Magic Roundabout was just almost eye-wateringly beautiful to watch. You could almost taste it.

Then later still.

There was a hierarchy of telly watching in our house, past seven o'clock.Rah, as she was older, had special privileges. 8:30 for her. 7:30 for me. Which made it sometimes difficult for me to go to sleep. Particularly if there was something forbidden on telly, like Not in Front of The Children. That title resonates particularly of course. I don't think I ever saw one whole episode. And, because that was the "Era of Deletion" I don't think I ever will.

Weekend evening viewing was utterly exotic.

When I was seven I was allowed to stay up until 8:30 on Friday nights. Stanley Baxter Show. I can remember the thrill – like I'd been summoned by The Chosen One. I still can't remember exactly why but there was something gilt-edged about Stanley Baxter – like you knew, even at that edge, that you were in the company of comedic genius. Or at least just something very special indeed.

Then Saturday and Sunday. The list is almost endless - Cliff Richard, Basil Brush, Cilla (her spoken voice much more appealing than her singing one), Lulu (had a thing for her for a while), Tom Jones and Englebert Humperdinck (interchangeable). Brucie. That was slightly later but still in the era. As was The Two Ronnies.

Mum and Da liked them. Weren't so keen on Morecambe and Wise. But we were.

I'm sure that the budgets were much narrower than today's but it all seemed so glitzy then. That's possibly because everything was properly in its place, with space around it. Everything was something you could see, something you could hear. All was clearer perhaps, better defined. From the signature tunes, to the received tones of the continuity announcers to the tarantaras of the show jingles, to the artistry of the cartoons.

Thing was, it didn't matter whether any of these things or people were funny, entertaining even, or not. They were there, that was all that mattered. You watched them because you watched them. It was the familiar, repeated format that kept you happy, not necessarily the content or quality of it. They said it how it was back then. Light Entertainment. The above - in two words.

All of these programmes felt like something, things that are difficult to put into words. They were physically warm, cold, scary, sexy. Some were unbearable, like Titch and Quackers. Ventriloquists' dummies did that to me. They were your night-mare monsters, come to life.

There were only three, sorry, 5 channels (well, maybe that's 3 plus a couple of "variations" as they used to say in the Radio Times) but it's true that there was a lot more on than now. Because it really did cover the gamut - the more narrow gamut we knew and appreciated, anyway. And because we weren't as spoiled we appreciated it more.

I had quite a thing for the Radio Times,. Always say I learnt to read from it. We used to get it every week, delivered. 5 days before the programmes actually went out, so I had a lot to look forward to.

I'd totally absorb it. I loved the covers, loved the layout of the schedules. I used to get mini-obsessed about really trivial things. Like the fact that it always said "Colour" next to certain programmes and not to others. That made them look more special somehow, more exotic. The fact that they were all in black and white on our set anyway made no difference. Well, maybe there were in fact more interestingly grey than the ones actually broadcast in black and white.

Or maybe I really am dressing up the past.

CHAPTER 16

Hello Samantha

Don't let anyone ever tell you that a six-or-seven year old doesn't get butterflies. *Particularly* a six-or-seven year old.

I met Samantha when she was 4. I was 5. It was the very first term at The School and I'd been especially selected by the powers that were to present a bouquet to the Headmistress, affectionately known by just about everyone as. Doris. Or Juicy. D'you see? Juicy Doris. Samantha was at the quaint wee version (yes, quaint and twee, as opposed to Glorious and Grand over the other end of town) of the primary part of The School over in Bear Flat, in the South West corner of the City. Lesley House, it was called. That's where sister Sarah went.

Samantha was my counterpart. Handing over a bouquet. Except of course, she was a girl. But then there weren't any boys at Lesley House. Ever. And I was the only boy in the Whole School. No, wait, there was a boy two years above me but you barely noticed him. So, as far as I was concerned, yes I was the only boy. Have I said that already? Silly me.

It was prizegiving. That time of the year when schools like this congratulated themselves on another year of achievement, achievement, more achievement. And survival. And strangely coiffed dignitaries. Like the fragrant Head Doris and her Special Guest Star. Possibly the Mayor's Wife. Or someone from the Girls' Public Day School Trust. With a Big Bosom. So I got the Head and Samantha got the Guest Star with the Big Bosom. We didn't really understand the seriousness of all this hoopla so we just got on with our respective jobs of delivering floral excesses and receiving pats on heads and special doggy biscuits.

It was all very, very serious. And absorbing seriousness at just-about-five is actually quite good fun. The gravity bonded

Samantha and me, no doubt about it.

This was the first time I got really nervous, I think. I'd been briefed, as had Samantha and we were ready for our first Important Civic Duty.

To the tune of Country Gardens. Of course! That was their school tune. And possibly school song. Though the history of it has slightly confused me. Did anyone actually ever sing it while I was there? I certainly never remember singing it myself. And it's possible that the only version that anyone actually knew had lyrics far too modern too have been adopted by the lofty administrators of Bankton High.

Not for the last time at The School, I had to wait at the bottom of some stairs in yet another strange, unknown building, this time with a stage. The stage was just over there and I was just over here, waiting with a rather small bouquet, as far as I remember. Quite a poor excuse for an offering, in retrospect. A posy, really, I suppose. Samantha the same. We were there for quite a long time. As far as I recall there were no actual prizes given out at all - it was just us, Doris and Doris's Dignitary. It was also a little bit dimly lit. It all seemed very 1960s, like before colour. Which it was, of course.

But we loved it. And what I really remember was just gassing - 5 year-old gas. The Herbs, those small flowers, shoes and why we both had to wear buckles. And our silly mummies. Their hair, mostly.

And when I first met Samantha she had short hair and could have been a pretty blond boy.

Then I met her again - this time when I was waiting in one of the side rooms at Lesley House, for Sarah to come out of class. It must have been the middle of Transition - perhaps at the end of the Spring Term.

She'd changed. And she was Gorgeous. In a seriously Gorgeous way. To this day I've never been so pole-axed by a blonde female as I was by her. Everything was perfect. Her voice, her gently beautifully framed face, her luscious (now THAT's a seventies word) long blonde hair. She was like one of the Harmony girls. Except she was 6. And she was funny. And kind.

We recognised each other immediately. Not bad, considering there'd been over a year and a half between then and Prizegiving. A year and a half for us was, after all, a third of a life away! We chatted, mostly about brothers and sisters, Banana Splits, whether she liked Lesley House ("It's alright"), Dr. Who, her house (it was too small for 5, I think she said) and Wacky Races. In that order. We must also have complimented each other on a few things. We were a polite and nice girl and boy, weren't we. And I probably fancied her. Though that was not a word I knew of course then. That feeling could be described as a tummy feeling or maybe a Sandra Dee Feeling.

Samantha was now officially really, *really*, nice.

And then I met her again. This time she'd come over with her classmates from Lesley House to check out the gargantuan Big School over the other end of town. Must have been the end of Summer Term 1971.

And this time she was mine. We already had our thing, our connection, the one we'd been nurturing all this time. Well, the previous two times. We just got on. Beautifully. And she was coming my way! For good! Because this time was the time when the quaint wee kids from the quaint wee house over the way had to leave the quaint wee house as the quaint wee house was being decommissioned by the school. So I was going to get Samantha every single day. For my third year at The School this was my very special prize at my own own very special prizegiving.

I think I'd deserved it. I'd put up with Nigel for a whole year and now I was going to get my just desserts. And so was he! When I saw her that time you might have just as well have slapped on some Donny then and there and let us disappear beyond the sunset. We talked. We held hands. We danced. Well, no we didn't actually. We kissed. Well, no we didn't do that either. But we talked and we held hands and that was enough for lovestruck 6-year-olds, down by the tennis court, talking about stuff and holding hands. Because that's what you do when you're six and in love. Or what you did then, anyway.

I never even suspected for a moment that we wouldn't be together every single day of the following year. Sharing special moments, a Rolo or two, never apart for a second. It was all so wonderfully, mesmerically mapped out.

I don't think we spent even a moment alone and together after that.

I like to think it was Nigel who was the culprit, the girl-thief. Maybe yes, maybe no. Maybe I just didn't have the staying power. Or maybe, in fact, and without even knowing it, I wasn't actually that interested after all.

Life can be blandly sad sometimes.

CHAPTER 17

Chirpy Bloody Cheep Cheep

Summer 1971 was "hotpaints". That's what I called them, anyway. Not that I was particularly interested in them. They were just there, or not, depending on your levels of prudishness.

More importantly, early Summer 1971 was Telly. And telly was Fab! The Banana Splits. Tra-la-la. God I loved the Banana Splits. Everything about them. Reassuredly goofy. Lots of variety for wandering minds. That kind of loopy magazine-y thing was totally up my street. And thousands of other kids. Mostly boys, I'd warrant.

Double Deckers was extraordinary too. Those kids on the bus. Where the heck were they going? Nowhere particularly but I thought it was absolutely gorgeous!

Summer 1971 was Gary. Not quite as successful as Tracey the year before. And certainly not as pretty. Or as yummy.

But I liked Gary. And he liked Popeye.

"I'm Popeye the Sailorman

I lives in a caravan

I opened the door

And fell on the floor

I'm Popeye the Sailorman"

"I'm Popeye the sailor man,

I lives in a caravan,

And when it gets chilly,

I tickle my willy,

I'm Popeye the sailor man."

"Toot! Toot!"

Don't think Popeye moved out of that caravan, all the time Gary was with us.

Gary was hard. He was nine and he was hard. But, unlike David the Demon Rock Thrower he was a Good Boy. Even Da could see that. Again, his family were all over the place. I remember we met his lot once, nearby in Bradford-on-Avon. They barely said a word. Must have thought we were bonkers, "looking after" Gary. We probably were. But he seemed to have fun with us, that summer.

Summer 1971 was also Scotland. Our continuing relationship with farmhouses. For the first time. Mrs. Maxwell, Mr. Maxwell and pig poo. Spoons with town crests on them. We bagsied our favourites - Galashiels, Berwick-upon-Tweed, Helensburgh. The fantastic smell of breakfast in the morning. Bacon. Old-fashioned bacon, with lots of meat, lots of gristle and lots of rind. Dinner in the evening. That stodgy, beefy, gravy smell.

Summer 1971 was Ponderax. Ponderax was a slimming pill. Actually, Ponderax were heaps and heaps of slimming pills. Ponderax belonged to Mum, who was concerned about her weight by 1971. Slimming pills were so much an early seventies thing. Small white smooth things they were. Mum took shed loads of them. Must have cost loads too. As good as eating chalk, they were.

Beautiful cities in the summer. Castle Douglas, Kirkcudbright (Kerk-oo-bree) and Dumfries. Beaches. Buckets and spades in abundance. To fill up the boot. Again. Just like last year. They did good beaches in South-West Scotland. We were warned of the pollution, for sure - a big thing in the seventies - but it was all good. Really good.

And comics. I ate comics. Big fat juicy summer bumper editions. Topper, Beezer, Cor!, Beano, Dandy. Shiver 'n' Shake and Whoopee!. No, maybe they came later. Loved them. New and funky. With loads of free gifts, like model planes and those helicopter thingies. Anyway, I had them all that summer. Beryl The Peril. Numskulls. Bash Street Kids. Remember the Kids had the perfectly drawn pie - could have eaten that pie. Such a disappointment to find it had a decoy frog in it.

Summer 1971 was also "trying to swim". I was rubbish at swimming. Was rubbish at most things sporty. Felt oppressed by sport, particularly stuff in water. It was ok, later, going with Dad when I could actually swim ok - well breaststroke anyway. But then it was not good. Still had water wings and the dreaded rubber ring.

Lessons were in the cold and clammy Royal Baths. These were, in the summer at any rate, outdoors. I swear they'd actually been used by the Romans, those baths. Crumbly bath stone surrounded you. And the water was pretty cold. The swimming teacher was an antiquity too. Miss Hathersage, I think. Complete dragon she was. Scared the living hell out of me. And anyone who scared me was highly unlikely to get anything good out of me, particularly anything exercise-y. I just froze.

I did manage to freak her, though. It's always the quiet ones. One day I grabbed a ring. Actually it was a inner tyre tube. Can't have been in water more than five feet deep, once I'd climbed in. I started on my pathetic paddle, gradually, tentatively across the vast expanse of the pool. Well, actually it was fifteen feet worth of vast expansiveness. To me I might as well have been cast overboard by Captain Pugwash and been splattering to safety, miles to go before the rocks devoured me.

Those inner tubes. Completely lethal. Over exertion and then... instant capsize.

It was clear that Miss Hathersage had not noticed me, at first. Apart from the occasional, menacing bark in my direction, that always seemed to be the case, in fact. Strange thing was, I was completely aware of everything and it all seemed to be going very slowly indeed. It seemed I was flipped upside down, under the water, for yonks. There wasn't much to see down there. All seemed a little mirky. And your hearing really does go like in the films, all gurgly-sounding. I did seem to be staring at the scene down there for a long time, to be sure. I could hear quite a lot of shouting above me. Then, suddenly, I felt a dramatic swelling beside be, like a tsunami or something and I was torn from the waters by what felt and smelled like a ferocious sea serpent.

Mrs Hathersage dragged me out of the pool. She was none too happy. "I TOLD you not to get into the RING BY YOURSELF! Go and get changed NOW!" Actually she was shaking. I think fear had made her angry. Not that I knew. Or cared.

Needless to say, my progress in learning how to be a fish was severely impeded by the experience. It'd be over two years before I ventured anywhere near the Royal Baths again. And certainly not in the company of Miss Hathersage.

Or was she Mrs?

Summer 1971 was also Chirpy Chirpy Cheep Cheep. That flippin' song was all over the place. Mostly on the radio and nearly as mostly sung by Nigel and his cousin Patrick. Constantly. "Whair-s ya mama gon, whairsyamama gonn!" "Faaar faar away". I was convinced that group were from the dustier parts of the deepest and dirtiest parts of America. Where they just cast their mamas and dadas away, without a care, to leave the liddle babbas to fend for themselves. The singer sounded like a Yankee mummy sheep, bleating her pain to anyone who cared to listen. And, let's face it, we all listened in the summer of 1971. All of us under seven, anyway. I really had no idea that they were a cutesy wee band from Scotland and that the lead singer looked like one of the younger (and not a little sexy) mums they had at The School. With hotpants of course.

CHAPTER 18

Who in Heaven's name is Jago?

Christmas is a festival none of us seem able to forget. Whoever we are and wherever we're from. Clearly I'm talking mostly about those of us who live in the West but it really does drive its point home. Mostly this is because of American influences, as per, but I wouldn't think it totally fair to blame whoever came up with Santa, Irving Berlin, Maceys, Coca-Cola or any other iconic modern symbol of Christmas. The story of the birth of Christ is as attractive as it's poignant, as are the cultural spin-offs. Personally I find it a little sad that we haven't all been imbued with a little more stories from other cultures but I guess it doesn't detract much from the fact that this side of Christmas, the spiritual side - that is, if you don't find watching White Christmas or It's a Wonderful Life re-runs equally as spiritual. Come to think of it...

Anyway, Christmas at 7 and 2 months meant as much to me as any Christmas had before it, if not more so. Because it marked my first brush with fame. As well as my first significant creative failure. Plus ça change, as you might say and, naturally, you'd be right.

By the end of the first half term of 1B I'd begun to get into my stride again, Nigel notwithstanding. In fact, for those first few weeks I'd say there'd been rather groovy harmony between us. Maybe not so much the Dynamic Duo - still a little Odd Couple - but, yes, groovy would be the word. He'd even lent me his Joe 90-mobile. That was almost Love, for Nigel.

As far as progress and all that stuff was concerned, I seemed to be getting along pretty groovily there too.

I was pretty much all grown up now. Getting to be trusted by the teachers to do some fairly ambitious things. Like sing solo.

And perform in a play. Without assistance.

At my daughter's nativity play a few year's ago - she was 10 - I was shocked - appalled even - to see the director - a form teacher, may even have been the Head - sit in front of the cast and mouth all the words to every bit of dialogue, every monologue, every solo, every ensemble piece. Dreadful behaviour - where's the adrenaline buzz in that. Where's the wow of tension? The feeling that you may faint before you even open your gob. Or wet yourself. There's nothing better than stage fright. It's essential to experience that first feeling of tense-tummy as early as you can. Of course it is.

With me - I was seven.

Now if we're going to get picky here and go as far as actually assessing the success of my first Big Performances, I'd say it was one screaming success and one unmitigated failure.

Let's start at the top, shall we?

A School Nativity Play.

Be honest. You remember your first Nativity Play, don't you? Now you've got children, you may not consider them overly important - maybe just an afterthought. Something, at best, you have to remember viz. cutting up sheets for shepherds' outfits or finding a stick in the garden and whittling it into a staff. Well, whatever you've had to do, it probably hasn't exactly warmed the cockles, has it? It's a necessary evil, yes? Like buying their uniform or remembering to donate just one cupcake for the Christmas raffle. But cast your mind back...

Wasn't your first Nativity Play the most enchanting, the most exciting, the most captivating thing you'd ever done? It's probably the first time you'd had make-up on your face, for a start. Or had not just one Yummy but an army of them fussing over you, to ensure you looked exactly the part that was chosen for you. Which could be anything of course, from the back of an ox to

Mary and Joseph themselves. Or the Three Kings.

Or, in my case, Jago.

You know Jago, of course you do. Jago, the young disciple of The Three Kings? I tell you now that he's quite possibly the most significant character in any of the Scriptures.

Jago was Welsh. Well, no he wasn't, he was Indian. Or Persian. Or maybe he was Arabian. But when I played him he was Welsh. Definitely. Shirley Bassey's son, possibly. Not that it mattered. Because it was, and possibly continues to be, my proudest moment on the stage. And I've trodden some boards, I can tell you.

We were sitting in the classroom one day, after lunch break, Nigel and I, together with the other girls. Miss McKay seemed to have something important to say. So we listened carefully as we were wont to do when She uttered. And what made it a little more intriguing than usual was the fact that She seemed to have another teacher to help her with Her announcement. She said, "We're casting an important role for our Nativity Play. This will be the only speaking part for someone in your Year. Now in order for you to get this important role you have to be able to do an accent".

"What sort of accent, Miss?" Nigel asked. "Well it's a character called Jago and he's the little friend of The Three Wise Men. So he has to have an accent from The Mystical East".

"What's that then, Miss?"

"Well, like Indian. You just have to read a couple of lines for us"

For some reason (I can't remember why, perhaps because they intended it to be one of the boys) they chose me to go first.

I looked down at the script. It said, "Is there anybody there?"

"Don't know if I can do Indian, Miss".

Quick as a flash, Nigel whispered.

"Do Welsh."

Now Nigel's mum, Eleanor, was Welsh. Very Welsh. From Cardiff, I seem to remember. Beautiful voice, as I recall. As I said, Dad was a great mimic and he had a lot of regional accents off pat, so I must have inherited a touch of that from him. Because almost as soon as I'd uttered "Is there anybody there" the whole class started sniggering. Except in a good way. It was Miss McKay and Miss Higgins' (yes, I think it was she had dep'd for the occasion) Eureka moment of the year, clearly. They both looked extremely pleased with themselves. Like they'd discovered the next Bobby Crush.

"Yes, yes, that's perfect. Congratulations. The part is yours"

And so it was that my first experience of an Acting Nature was in December 1971. In the School Hall. As a blacked-up Arabian-PersianIndian person. With Welsh accent.

I remember going in early. The tension and the excitement. In amongst the Grown Up Girls, in the Grown Up School. Going into one of the Big Girls' classrooms - a makeshift dressing room - for costume and make-up. And a woman I'd never see again being very kind and inquisitive and excited for me. And the extraordinary mingling of estrogen and a variety of eaux de toilette.

We came up there every year at about this time, for the Nativity. Kindergarten had been all Away in a Manger and Little Jesus Sweetly Sleep and was Old Corridor Smells and Feeling the Warmth of The Girl Gang, in a row, singing in that slightly out-of-tune, slightly wordless and dream-like way that young children do.

Transition was the same sort of thing, I think. Can't really remember it. The pleasure of it was being in the group, The Team, singing for your supper. Sort of.

This time I was on my own, Kid. This was my moment. My

coming Claim to Fame.

I was barely 7 and running Solo. This was it. Down by the stairs at the bottom of the stage. Thinking of the first line. The first line I'd first seen as the first words, the words that had brought me here. What were they again?

The assembled cast of Mary, Joseph, The Angel Gabriel, Head Shepherd, a couple of stray kids and (probably) a donkey exited stage left.

Enter Peter, stage right. Up the stairs. Advanced acting, on the way up the stairs, saying "Is there anybody there?" Moving across the stage now, saying to the audience - blinded by the lights - "Is there anybody there?".

Silence.

Then hysteria. No. Really. Hysteria. Three hundred men, women and children. In hysterics.

A little boy. Blacked up. Looking every inch the errant Pakistani. Little Chap. Speaking Welsh. Quite convincingly too. Look you.

I think it took them over 3 minutes to settle down.

I think I probably fluffed a couple of lines. That became a recurring habit over the years. Not that it mattered, this first time. I'd made my mark. As a special privilege, what's more, I got to sing the descant part in O Come All Ye Faithful. "Sing Choirs of Angels, sing (up the register, Special Girls) in ex-ul-tay-shon". Now that really was special.

Christmas would never be quite the same again.

Three weeks later and Miss Mmm-Lovely rightly thought I was on a roll and, fully expectant that I would capitalise on my now-legendary performance, asked me to sing a duet with a Rising Starlet in the year above, for a special Carol Concert taking place in front of the school, the day before Break Up.

"Take this carol and learn it. You're the Page. Sally's the King. Make sure that you get in touch with her well before the performance. You'll need to rehearse of course. Take this..." she handed me the words "and LEARN YOUR LINES".

Sally was in the year above. And very confident she was too. I think she was considered the shining star of 1A, or 1 Removed as it was sometimes called. God knows why it was called that. Anyway, Sally was a Prima Donna and she wasn't too chuffed that she had a partner. Good King Wenceslas was not a good choice, as far as she was concerned.

It was all pretty clear. "Page" was written clearly beside the lines I was supposed to learn, "King" besides Sally's and "Both" where we were to deliver together.

Another success in the offing.

Except that... Sally wasn't playing. No way, not with a little erk like me. Not with someone from the year below. And certainly not with a boy!

So, when I went up to her and suggested we trot off like the Chosen Two - Glyn Poole and Bonnie Langford - she huffed a certain amount and said "Don't think so. I'll meet you in morning break just before the performance."

Looking back, I know I should have put my size twelves children's size down but we were dealing with royalty here. What's more and as I've already said I always seemed to be struck dumb by older girls.

So morning break it was. And I really hadn't prepared. Sally sensed this and breezed sunnily through the whole rehearsal, completely ignoring me of course.

So. There we were. Standing next to each other. She occasionally poking me in the ribs. I liked to think at the time they pokes of encouragement but, as per Patricia, I never suspected foul play.

And then.

The moment came.

Girls, girls, girls. And a fair smattering of jolly parents, girded for their imminent pleasure.

"Good King Wenceslas, sung by Sally and Peter"

Round of applause. Fair sized one as it happened. Good start.

Can you see where we're going with this?

First verse fine. Sang together and in any case, everyone knows the words to the first verse!

"Gath'ring wint-ter phew oo well!"

Done - getting into my stride.

Next bit was Sally's. Totally in the moment. Silly cow.

"Hither, page, and stand by me

If thou know'st it, telling

Yonder peasant, who is he?

Where and what his dwelling?"

Then it happened. An honest moment. Just at the wrong moment.

I decided that I hadn't after all prepared at all for this. Had not bothered. Or forgotten. Or perhaps thought that after my triumph as Jago I was invincible. And I'd suddenly realised I wasn't. And that, consequently, it was my moment. My moment all right. To suffer.

I could have at least imagined the words. Or something. Sung a different song. Maybe my version of Chirpy Chirpy Cheep Cheep. The Pinky and Perky one. Or done a jig. But no.

I nearly made it on that first Page's retort. Tried. Just a little.

Piano.

Page's Silence.

More silence from the Page.

Audience starts to shuffle.

And yet more piano.

And yet more silence from the Page.

And a little coughing now.

"...by St. Agnes' Fountain"

Like a shimmering, er, fountain, it came to me. Quite a visual boy I was.

The sighs of relief were palpable. Little did they know that visual recognition had by now long passed and I was, as they say on these infamous occasions, on my own. Blank canvas. Devoid of snow, footsteps, fountains, anything.

Sally was by now anything but Good. Changed mood and changed sex. Now she was Evil Queen.

The next verse came out as nothing less than a ranting threat.

"*Bring* me *flesh* [yours preferably] and bring me wine [your blood of course]

Bring me pine logs hither (visions of a shackled slave no doubt, with wood splintering my back)

Thou and I will see him dine [on your carcass - and I, for my part, will savour this cannibalism]

When we bear him thither."

Of course I could do the next bit...

"Page and monarch forth they went

Forth they went together

Through the rude wind's wild lament

And the bitter weather"

...and the following verse, well, lip-synch almost as well as Marc Bolan, as Sally was singing heartily by now of course - reminding me now again not so much Good King W, more Bad King Henry 8, accompanied as she / he was now by a few of the honorary choir girls / henchmen. And Miss M' Och Aye.

I never recovered. The next verse was utterly Page Free and Piano Solo, despite being the best opportunity yet this young performer had had to shine and further cement his Superstar status.

But they do (or possibly might) say that a Superstar is only as good as his last line. And I'd now fluffed 12 of mine so the Stage that I'd so successfully upped everyone on not three weeks previously had now swallowed me whole.

But not before the final ignominy of Diva Sally, now rather surprisingly transformed into Captain Mainwaring and her last two words. All together now.

"Stupid Boy".

A PTTV PRODUCTION

Sing a song, Peter

I'm a little tree
Petey tree
Swinging in the breeze
Fighting off the fleas

I'm a little tree
Look at me
Standing small and free
Nature's mini key

What I love is unknown
People come and go
Playing in the meadow
And the un-der-growth

What I have is mine
Something quite divine
Absolutely nothing
Can be un-der-mined

I'm a little tree
Little Petey green
Brown and quite serene
Sway but never lean

I'm a little tree
Look at me
Absolutely, totally
Completely free

CHAPTER 19

Top of the Popsicles

Sweets. Mum said she never gave us any.

That's a bit like saying she never inhaled when she smoked.

I ate loads of sweets and things like that. And lots of salty things. All manner.

Dib-dabs. Sherbert dips. Wasn't so keen on them - the liquorice of course. Who really liked liquorice. Really? Those tri-coloured solid lollies. Loved them. What else? Ah - Lovehearts of course. Refreshers - Lovehearts' poor relation. Spangles.

Lollipops. Humbugs. Rather liked butterscotch.

Kit-kats. All those biscuit-y things with caramel insides. Slightly later on - Curly Wurlies. Flakes. Ripples - though I always thought they were a bit more exotic.

Liked lollies too. Particularly anything orange. And occasionally things like Zooms. And Milky Ways and Milky Bars, for the same reason. Didn't like Mars bars. They were boring - too much of a basic bar. Too rudimentary for us sophisticated sweet eaters.

And car sweets. Though they were a bit weird. Why would you have sweets just for the car? In an old tin? With that weird sugary coating?

Smiths Crisps. Roast chicken flavour probably my favourite. Quavers. Twiglets. Amazing what's still around. And what's not.

Most of what I liked was pretty much determined not so much by my peers as by the ads on the telly. Ads were great. Very exotic. I was one of their moths.

Mum was very proud of the fact that she didn't let us have any sweets. She thought that and the fact that we had the best dentist in the West of England was why we all had such great teeth.

I was just lucky with my teeth. Simple as that.

Granddad always used to carry packets of sweets around with him. Religiously. Polos. Occasionally Trebor mints but mostly Polos. But always mints. Was always handing them out.

Granddad was Dad's Dad. He was so completely Granddad that we really didn't need any other grandparents.

Firstly, he had a Granddad name. Norman. Secondly, his was a proper age for a Granddad - 80 when I was 4.

He shuffled. Of course he shuffled but he was also pretty active.

And totally regimented. Utterly organised. Never out of time, was Granddad. Always the same.

He always arrived on the same Black and White coach from Milnrow, on the outskirts of Manchester, exactly 8 1/2 hours away.

He always brought with him the same box of stiff collars (though possibly not the same collars). And the same styled Granddad white shirt, with those sleeve stays that he used to push up to the top of his arms. He always wore cufflinks. He always wore the same kind of grey suit. Baggy trousers with always the same braces.

Same shaving brush, same shaver. Same toothbrush.

Same hairbrushes. He had two ivory handled "Men's hairbrushes" that you used to push together and he'd brush his temples with both brushes at the same time. Come to think of it, I think Dad had the same type of hairbrushes.

Used to get up at the same time every day. 7:30. Got on Mum's nerves, when he was staying.

He used to tell the same stories - the same nursery rhymes, with the actions. "There was a little girl and she had a little curl...". "Doctor Foster went to Gloucester". "This is the way the farmer rides. Hobbledy hoy". He always used to tell us the same true story of when he was in The Great War, in The Trenches, about one of the privates pretending to be a little boy and up-setting the officers. Can't quite remember it but it was funny. And sad.

He'd always bounce you up and down on his knee, or swing you through his legs, by the arms. Granddads did that then. Noone raised an eyebrow. Why should they have? There was no reason to. None.

I think he treated all children the same, the same, that is, until they were 9. Then he'd change. I can remember him getting quite cross with me when I was about 10. Can't quite remember why - must have been how I was behaving towards Sephie.

He had incredibly clear views about how to raise kids. He probably had a view about a little boy being sent to a girl's school, though he never let me know it of course.

He had a unique gift with children. His gift was to behave exactly the same way every time because he knew, instinct-ively, that all children love repetition. Repetition in stories, jokes, habits, love. These are the stories, jokes, habits and love that he knew helped shape their world. I'm sure he knew how re-sponsible his Granddad job was and how influential.

Yes - our Granddad was straight and true. The very best Granddad you ever knew.

CHAPTER 20

Sexy itch

What's that feeling you get when you're so young. Is it the collywobbles? Is it butterflies. The whoosh? Is it sexual? Or just exciting? Forbidden?

Or is it all these things?

One day, Nigel and I were playing in the bit down by the crescent hill near the front entrance by Lansdown Hill. The bit near the swings. It was about 5 minutes in to lunch break and we were probably just talking about stuff. Maybe Nigel's new Matchbox racing track or his new cars or his Joe 90 mobile. Or something. Funny thing was that at that age, in the girl's school, there wasn't anything like a football to knock about. Or a tennis ball to throw. Or anything sporty. It was a Girl's School, Juicy.

Anyway, suddenly out of the corner of my eye came a throng. I think that's what you'd call it. Not really a gang. More a throng. Of older girls, year above I think. And they'd been at the rose hip bushes down along the edge of the crescent. Because they'd discovered something rather interesting about the rose hips, those intense red oblong-shaped fruits that almost look good enough to eat but you can kind of tell, even at that age, that they're too intense, too plant-y to dare tasting.

That's funny. It's that prickly feeling again. Just thinking about them makes me itch.

Yes, of course. The little minxes had discovered the joys of itching powder. And they were on a prank. A big one.

They were Itching Powder Ringleaders. And they were rounding up the younger kids and giving them merry red hell.

And Nigel and I got caught. But separately. And held ransom.

And I don't mind saying that it was flipping fantastic.

Later when I was about 12 there was proper bullying along the canal to contend with. Only time in my life in fact. Of that kind.

But here. This was different. It was threatening but in an entirely different way. Of course, we didn't want to succumb to The Itch. Very unpleasant - or at least that's what it seemed like. They'd already got some of our class mates and they seemed in a bit of a state. It didn't seem like itching powder to us - more like The Plague. Lunchtime Plague.

Nigel and I both, held captive in different hedge hideouts, bush bases, were rather enjoying ourselves, negotiating with our captors.

They were rather attractive I thought. And they were enjoying the goading. So were we.

Was this the beginning of something masochistic? If so, it's probably the only experience of it I've had in my life. And at 7? No, seems unlikely.

What I think it was, now, was an early experience of flirtation. We were flirting with the girls with the itching powder. And they in their turn were flirting back. By threatening but not actually carrying out the Application of The Powder.

So, yes it was a bit sexual. And threatening. But it certainly wasn't bullying. It was almost benign. Like they were giving us a treat. The treat, or thrill of fending off imminent itchiness. By chatting. Or back-chatting, perhaps. Something like this.

"I will, I will"

"No you won't. Of course you won't. You'll get caught and told off and probably your Dad will get angry. And your mum"

"No they won't. They're never angry with me," Girl 1 said. Susannah?

"Never angry with me neither," said Girl 2. "They think I'm lovely".

"Well maybe they think you're lovely", I said. "Maybe you are". Smiling.

A pause, then a smile back.

"But you're going to get it. And we're going to give it to you."

"No you're not"

"Yes we are"

I was so loving this. I wanted it to go on all term. All year, if possible.

Then the bell rang.

For some reason that experience, the thrill of being chased, caught and tormented, deliciously, never came again.

Even in the disco. Or village hall. Or club. Or pub. Or wine bar.

Or at home.

CHAPTER 21

Bloody Bath

It was funny because Mum used to talk to me like an adult, even when I was seven. Not that I necessarily noticed. I just remember that we'd talk about absolutely everything.

One thing we talked about was what Mum actually thought of Bath. By 1972 anyway.

Bath, as many will tell you, is a beautiful city. Now, that is. Now it's had its heart put back.

It's not just the status of World Heritage Site. Or the fact that it was Britain in Bloom winner for so many years in succession the organisers decided to ban Bath effectively for life from entering. It's that, finally, someone has had the sense to realise that, in Bath, you really don't mess with the past. And, architecturally at least, there have been two Epochs of Beauty - Roman and Georgian.

So, in the 1960s, when town planners seemingly decided to take as many drugs as were going down over there in Cosmic Cosmopolitan Counterculture, those indulgent buggers really did do a big dump on the place.

They tore out the beautiful Victorian shops (yes, they were Victorian and beautiful too) along the southern part of the city and replaced them with the weirdest, dullest, most inappropriately low-slung monstrosities ever devised. And stretched them out for about one square mile. And they put them next to the already shameful early-sixties horrors that housed the technical college students and their civil service counterparts.

Yes, late-sixties Britain really was beige. And central Bath was beigest, once they'd done the do in 1972 when the Blow of Baddest Taste had been landed.

Not that the Bathonian Snobburghers didn't deserve it of course. Of course they did. They deserved it unreservedly. Filthy materialists, every man John and woman Jacqueline of them. More money than sense. Admiralty types. Advertising types. Nouveaus. Accountants. In high proportion. Living bang smack next to low-income menial workers who must have thought they were living in Armageddon. OK, Twerton then.

How do I know this? Mum. She hated it. Hated them. Not because they had money. More because they were a bunch of unfriendly toss-pots (one of Dad's), born into money and whisked off this mortal with more than pots of it. Not that Mum didn't have her own particular aspirations. A bigger, more stately home than we deserved to dream of (if you go by affordability at any rate) - that was her doing. And a lifestyle that betrayed her innermost feelings to the power of 3. The WI. Cleaners. Gardeners. Delivered laundry. 2 cars (well, maybe 2 cars was more common then). Trips to the hypermarket for more trinket-y antiquities. Audrey. Mozart. Bath Festival. The Ballet. Then Audrey again.

And the shops. Food shops where you ordered whatever then had it delivered. Shops where you bought the biggest, juiciest joints of the finest beef. I seem to remember this was the time when beef was fast becoming an inordinately expensive luxury. Shops where there were always people with aprons and, occasionally, hats. Shops where things smelt. And smelt good. Like jelly. Why doesn't jelly smell anymore? Then there were the shops where women went to dress. Shops like Jaeger. Jaeger was patently the most expensive shop for almost anything anywhere in the world. And Mum could rarely afford to buy the left sleeve, let alone the whole jacket.

But she persevered, kept up appearances, paid for the posh shopping at Caters, paid for the Bolloms truck coming down the drive, and, yes, even paid for that Jaeger jacket, eventually. Despite Dad's protestations to the contrary. We were, after all, living off Mum's legacy and he (not her, strangely) felt protective towards it. And feeling bad that she couldn't really afford to live as she wanted to, because he really couldn't earn that kind of money, working where he did.

And did we have cleaners? Yes. Of course we had cleaners.

After we'd had cleaners I felt bad about having cleaners. Became a bit of an inverted snob. Seems a little silly now. Everyone needs to work, after all. Or is it encouraging subservience? Still unsure.

Anyway, I didn't object to it then of course. In fact I found our cleaners, if not exactly exotic (that would have been weird) then pretty interesting people.

Mrs. Huxtable and Mrs. White.

They were old. In the case of Mrs. White, very old I think. Of course, more people were old then than now. I was five after all. My folks were however much older than your average Kindergarten-er's folks - by about ten years, as I think I've already mentioned - so old was probably nearer to what I thought was old at the time than I possibly remember. Mrs. White was knocking eighty in fact. Not bad, to be getting around and about and up the stairs crouching over the little hoover. Or cleaning the floors. Mrs. White didn't wear a white coat to do the cleaning. Or maybe she did. She was very little, I remember, stick-like, wizened. Got into all the corners, all the nooks and crannies. Very good indeed. Lived on Widcombe Crescent. We went to see her, Mum and I, a few times, when she'd retired for good. Made tea for us, with Nice biscuits and Bourbons. Very creaky Bath accent. Strong as a a fox, though and just as wily.

Mrs Huxtable was younger. And rounder. Friendly but not as genuinely so as Mrs. White. She was good at the Brasso. Always had the cutlery out. Think she considered it an art form.

I really got on with these two, as I had got on with Mrs Johnson before them, when we lived in Gloucestershire, where the Missing Links lived.

And I think it's what's given me a healthy respect for people not fortunate enough (do I mean that?) to have had the kind of upbringing I've had. In fact, I'd go as far to say that I've always got on much better with someone who's Working Class than someone who's Middle. Can't say I've met many barons, earls or any other kind of peer for that matter so Upper has never come into it. Not unless you count those present at fetes, the theatre or some other public place where you were offered their flesh to press as a token gesture of intimacy.

No, White and Huxtable were good eggs, definitely. They both kept me entertained and I never really bored of them. They were also kind, which fitted in well with all the other sisters, (well maybe not sisters), cousins, aunts and other well-wishers commonplace at that time.

So Mum became a bit hung-up about Bath. Because she was growing to detest the place. And because she wanted to have everything it offered. And perhaps the most hung-up thing she did was in fact a hung-up thing.

Pastels were in then. Not just Rowntrees Fruit Pastels. Pastels, the kind with which you drew, coloured, painted, whatever the expression is. They made everything look like some sort of washed out cartoon. Real paint gave texture and life to every-thing. Paint came back, of course but for now most paintings were pastelings. And they stank.

It was coming up for Dad's 50th. This was a big deal, though presumably Dad didn't actually give two hoots. Mum decided to do something really special. A picture - yes, definitely a pic-ture. A portrait of the the darling children. And Mum knew just the person. It was the friend of one of the neighbourhood chat-terers. She was a fairly well-known local artist. That, of course, meant nothing to me. It was the equivalent of getting me to go and see a play at the Theatre Royal in town - no one famous so it'd be rubbish, then.

This, of course, meant that we would have to what they called "sit". I imagined we'd have to be trained like John's dog, Shep..

The artist, I think, was called Joanna. She lived up close to the school, which was fairly convenient of course, for me and for Sarah. And Seph of course went everywhere with Mum.

Her sitting room was a very typical sitting room, I remember, in the sense, I suppose, that every sitting room was typical back then. Patterned settees, two of them, upholstered in that brush fabric, a kind of greeny-puce colour. Coffee table, button-back chair. We sat on one of the settees. No, that's not right. Sarah sat on the settee and Seph and I were told to stand, either side, like she was our dowager aunt or mummy or something weird like that.

Anyway, it was slightly painful and rather dull. Strangely, I rather liked the finished product, when it finally appeared, some 6 months after our first sitting. I'm sure paintings don't always take that long but for a very long time afterwards I imagined that most portraits were painstaking, laborious affairs which took forever.

I say "strangely I liked it" because it was very bad. Very bad indeed.

When the much-awaited (by Mum and us at any rate) moment came at Dad's party Mum had made a big deal of it. She'd invited the whole family, of course - that was most of the Beaconsfield, Gerrards Cross, Twickenham, Teddington and all points South-west and West of London lot. As well as the Rochdale, Milnrow, Altrincham and all points North-west of Manchester lot. And they all came, every one of them, such was Dad's enduring, endearing popularity. And they all waited patiently while people gathered from outside (it was a very pleasant Spring day in March) and crammed into the sitting room. Dad had cottoned on to the fact that he was about to unveil something. I think he sensed something slightly unsavoury lurked underneath because he seemed a little nervous. Naturally enough, his "Now I'm 50" speech was as funny and self-deprecating as any other he'd made. Not that I'd heard any of course. I just sensed it. He was just a very, very funny man, particularly amongst his own, however much he always seemed to be reluctant to appear before them all.

Anyway, he paused for a while, having uttered, and looked at the piece of material hanging over the picture frame. Finally he pulled. And pulled a rather sheepish grin.

To say the final portrait bore absolutely no resemblance to any of us would be something of an understatement. I had, of course, been forced into my suede patchwork waistcoat thing so looked fairly ridiculous anyway. At least I wasn't wearing shorts. Cords, though and they looked very grey on the pastel painting for some reason, even though they were light blue. My face looked uncommonly ruddy, a bit like Joe - the cartoon Joe. Yes, I looked like Cartoon Joe. Sophie looked like a lifeless dolly or maybe "frozen" is a better word. Sarah looked about 20 years older and, what was that? A moustache had appeared on her top lip. Frightening.

Mum loved it, of course. No one else passed comment. Dad never said a word.

I might not always have got on with Dad but there was rarely a time when I didn't admire just about everything he was thinking. And his sense of humour, expressed or otherwise, got me every time.

He was also a man of particular taste. Which meant that a) he was difficult to please and b) what he liked he completely adored.

So here two things were tested. His taste and sense of humour.

It was, after all, a personal landmark for him, no matter how hard he found to accept it as anything other than just another day. The day itself he'd been quite affected by. All his family was here and he was enjoying their company greatly. And of course Mum had organised all of it.

Dad, despite his legendary marriage, got pissed off with it all later in life. But at least, unlike me, he could say that the distinctly uncomfortable "50" was a great moment for him - possibly his zenith.

And in amongst this, this was a big gesture, one of the biggest Mum had ever attempted with an effort that had been as big as the momentous occasion she'd imagined.

So his bourgeois sense of taste and his humour were pressed to such an extent that he nearly burst that day. Maybe he felt that this represented how far Mum and he had drifted.

But 50's a funny time. I'm sure, as I move headlong through this unsettling time to its imminent arrival, that it's possibly as cathartic a time as any. Momentous in the changes it affects. Like attitude. Some say a resignation. Others say a peaceful acquiescence.

And I'm sure on that day back in March 1972 Dad felt a kind of mirthful peace, something that trumped his feelings of disappointment, distaste and fear.

It was, after all, the thought that counted.

CHAPTER 22

Please don't poison the children

I remember food. Food, hideous food. And milk.

Oh God That Milk!

Every morning, the crate arrived with those little silver top mini bottles, all ready to dullify the little girls' lives.

Not sure whoever had the idea of milk. It had been available to schools since 1921. It was considered important as a welfare issue because apparently it had been proven that kids from lower income families were more malnourished compared to their more upper class counterparts. So it was thought that a bottle of cold watery milk would do the trick. A bit of protein and fat would sort the poor wee kids out.

Which would have been ok of course except for the fact that that milk was horrid. And of course you had to drink it. Those were the days of not talking back - for anything - unless you were in the gravest danger, or something.

Cold, watery protein and fat. That was about the size of it. Particularly horrid on a cold day in December. And unlike Nursery School, you didn't get the milk biscuits to go with it.

I wish I'd rebelled. I wish I'd had the devil-may-care adventurousness of a spoilt wee bugger. And risked everything. It would have been worth it. Because the memory of that cold tasteless liquid, emulsifying my tongue, then my innards, and doing nothing else except freezing just about every organ inside me, makes me shiver now.

Hooray to the senseless Tory bastards who got rid of it. It's maybe not the greatest good deed an Administration can be remembered for but I'm grateful to them anyway.

For the most part, The School was Lovely, as I said. For the most part, because, apart from the occasional smack, there was a recurring, unavoidable terror that occurred every day for three years. At about 12:30. Lunch. Hideous, almost without exception.

You got used to most of it of course. The arid chocolate sponge with insipid "chocolate" sauce. The spam which made most of us want to heave. And some of us did. The inexplicably tasteless, clumpy mash. And. And. Oh no! The horrific, monstrous liver.

You had to eat up. No choice. It's the only time Miss McKay became the Wicked Witch of the West, the Mean Lunch Queen supplanted into the Music Angel. She hung over you, haranguing you with "Finish it! I don't care what it tastes like. Finish it now or they'll be hell to pay." Occasionally, when a courageous Miss had the audacity to slip the liver behind the radiator, smacks would be dispensed with ardent vigour. Needless to say, I was never that brave.

So, we'd traipse up to no. 12 Lansdown Crescent, which would be my sister's residence while I was in 1B (Sarah was 10, nearly 11, so that made her really quite old - nearly in the Big School), traipse back down the steps to what seemed sometimes like the deepest darkest dungeon but which was in fact rather an attractive room in a particularly splendid Georgian terraced house. Then eat the worst, barely edible, crud ever to to pass the lips of a wee kiddie. Eeewwww, as they might say now. Then we'd traipse back upstairs and back down again to the main school , our stomachs leaden with non-nutrients.

That said, two rather marvellous things happened (one of them on a fairly regular basis) in those Draconian lunchtimes.

Firstly, the coming of The Salvation Orange. It remains to this day the most beautiful fruit ever. Why? Because this was our pudding treat, every 2 weeks, on a Friday. It seems incredible now that the common-or-garden orange would ever be considered quite such a Godly fruit but what there was to compare it with was so extremely revolting that it shone like a golden orb in a cesspit.

The second thing was that I learnt to, well not exactly love but maybe "respect" The Liver.

Nigel had a calm contempt for food. The only use for it, as far as he was concerned, was to manipulate parents.

He knew Mum hated little boys who didn't eat up. So he made sure that every time he came round he wouldn't. Then he'd ask for more. Interesting ploy, really. Then he'd get more. And not eat it. Think he had a total of six fish-fingers once and only managed to eat two. Well, one and a half - think he gave the other half to Ginger.

"Do you like chicken?"

"No"

"Carrots?"

"No"

"Tomatoes?"

"No"

He liked jelly of course. And ice cream of all flavours and dubious colours.

Green things that grew he would not touch. Particularly beans, the stringy variety. Curiously, baked beans was one of his favourites but only on thin white toast.

"He's so spoilt, that boy!"

The one thing he loved, above all else, was liver. How strange is that? Liver, the most hideous meat ever known. Well, liver as cooked by the lovely dinner ladies at The School.

Step 1: Take a piece of pig's liver

Step 2: Turn the industrial oven to hottest

Step 3: Fry liver for 10 minutes in lard

Step 4: Transfer to oven and cook for a further 20 minutes until dark grey

Step 5: Liver must be similar texture to your Startrite shoes. And about as hard-wearing.

Step 6: Cut into extremely small chunks to prevent instant indigestion from occurring

Step 7: Chew very slowly

Step 8: Spit out in disgust

But Nigel loved it. Which just goes to show how utterly perverse a little six year-old he was.

And, even more perversely, I grew to love it too, courtesy of Nigel.

Maybe it's because, very secretly, I looked up to him a little, I took his word that "liver's great. I love it. I'll have yours if you like". So I acquired its taste, almost immediately. It really was the driest, toughest, greyest liver ever tasted. Amazing what you can do if, lemming like, you follow your peers.

Then, after lunch, The Rug.

That was always a strange thing. The rug. Sort of a Tartan red and black thing.

Blanket? Not quite. Not really. It was a rug. And we had to get it ready every day for about 2 years, walk upstairs to form 1B and sit on it. For an hour. Compulsory nap time, that's what it was.

Why was that? It was only midday! And although most of us girls, up until the age of 5 perhaps, had always taken a nap at about 3, that didn't last long, even in 1972.

It certainly wouldn't happen today, even with the overly nurturing society we appear to live in. Sorry, completely appropriately nurturing society we appear to live in.

Every day then, at about 1:00, after the Hideous Lunch, we'd get trotted in and told to sit down, completely silently. We were encouraged to nap but were allowed to read if we wanted to. Despite the fact that I seemed to devour the learning-to-read books at school, reading books was not becoming a favoured pastime.

Comics, though, that was another thing. My relationship with Graphic Pulp started right there. But because I was a Girl, even my comic reading choices were a little perverse. So though I didn't nick Bunty and give it a good dolly-ogle, I did read Disneyland.

I was the perfect age to read it when it came out - six. The Disney studios were coming to the end of their Golden Era. Not that I had a view then of course. It was that I just loved that 101 Dalmatians stuff, The Jungle Book, The Aristocats, then Bedknobs and Broomsticks and Robin Hood. It was quirky, fun, escapist and the music was great too. So those wee comics were a great way of keeping all that stuff with me. Later still there'd be Beezer, Dandy, Beano, Whizzer and Chips, Topper, Cor!. Not so Namby-Pamby-Girlie-Disneyland.

Must've been Nigel's influence. Or something more sinister.

CHAPTER 23

What are you aiming at, Peter?

It's something I've rarely ever thought about. Most of my thoughts up until recently – the ones I remember - have been about relationships, mostly with the opposite sex. Yearning. Could be my middle name.

The fact is, though, that there never was any sport. Not that I remember. I think there may have been hula-hooping once. I think it was an older girl - think she could the whole cahula-boodle That bit where you whip it round, it goes forward, then comes back, like a Tonka Toy in reverse. Or keeping it, and ten others (I think it was ten, anyway) hul-ing (or is that hooping?) for ever and ever.

I remember the place where the rest of the school did netball. Can't ever remember playing it myself though.

I can't see why children as old as seven never seemed to get any competitive - or other, for that matter - strenuous exercise. Maybe because none of the teachers, Mrs. Thompson being perhaps a notable exception, ever seemed the right shape. Or age.

But there we were. And that's the way it was. I'm not lying and not playing games with my memory bank when I say, quite irrefutably, that the only competitive game I ever played in school was, yes, tiddly winks. Not ever marbles got a look in. Or conkers. Conkers was what I played badly with Nigel, outside of school.

And yet, and yet Nigel never seemed to be affected by any of the "no games" stuff at all. Not at all. Not at all whatsoever. It's extraordinary, really, that Nigel appeared in any way boyish at all. He was subjected to exactly the same cotton wool-ing that I was, in many ways more so, considering his super-doopermolly-coddling at home. Maybe that was it. He was so used to getting his way that he really did have supreme confidence in himself - something I never had. Because I never really got anything I desired.

Because, you see, I desired nothing. You want for nothing, there's nothing to want. You're unwittingly helpless and hopeless. If, however, and like Nigel, you get everything you want, you continue to desire and continue to get. Nigel's competition was with "more". He challenged more, he took more on. And he won. Yes, wanting more is akin to greed, gluttony, sloth and all that devilish stuff but it's still more healthy than wanting for nothing.

Oh teams of parents and little children, of whatever state of pleasure, pain or annoyance. Please remember. It is better to be entirely spoiled or completely devoid of owt than to be that awkward thing in the middle, which as you get older and more hoary you can put a name too. I like to call it "desire deprivation". A lack of desire when you're young has the doubly ironical effect of making you want more - regret causes that - and that, of course, makes you less cool, less desir-able. Lack of desire leads to desperation leads to... where?

CHAPTER 24

Bribes and prizes

Matchbox multi-storey carpark. A black and white plastic football. £30. 50p.

I wouldn't go as far as saying that my relationship with Nigel was based on money. Well, not that far anyway. Fact was, his parents were rich and mine weren't. And they gave him almost anything he wanted (and he certainly wanted). Come to think of it, they actually gave him everything he wanted. It's just that occasionally they made it seem like he was being called on to strive for it or that maybe it came as a kind of reward. Like taking the entrance exam to St. Thomas's School.

The first thing I remember about St. Thomas's Junior School was its prospectus. It looked so old, venerable and somehow far off or lofty. In retrospect it's probably because they hadn't updated it since the mid-fifites and all the boys had shiny flat hair and their clothes were grey and white. Come to think of it, everything was grey and white. In any case, I thought it looked as unreachable a place as anywhere described in The Phantom Tollbooth or Hatty Town.

You were taught subjects there. Things like English, Maths, Science. They even taught French there. A language - now that was exotic. And everyone looked so earnest, so severe. It looked foreboding but it looked fantastic, somehow. It was a place where you might be elevated to something seriously special. If you were special enough in the first place, of course.

To get in you had to do something called an exam. Now I knew about tests. I think we might have had a spelling test once at The Girls School. I think I did pretty well at that. Though for me the biggest achievement was becoming a probationer in the school choir. At long last.

Of course I think they did this to make me feel better. I had, after all, just 6 weeks to go before Summer Term and The End of School. Miss MMMM had an announcement, like she did every half-year, to say who was in and... well, she didn't exactly say who was out but it was as if she had. Everyone wanted to be in the choir. Not just because it was a MissM-endorsed activity but because it was a Big Serious Thing to do with something everybody loved - singing. So *not* being in the choir was something I'd been most disappointed about at The Girls School.

So being a boy at a girl's school had its disadvantages, in more ways than just being a boy. And this was the single most discriminatory - actually maybe the only discriminatory - act I experienced while I was there. In any case, a young boy like me would never have so much as felt discrimination, unless it was an act of cruelty or particular unfeeling. No - this was Bankton High and, Nigel-related events occasionally excepted, I'd had a beautiful time, I really had.

Maybe I had been judged on merit. Was I always out of tune? Too shrill? Just not coloured enough? I've always considered myself to be pretty musical and my voice is, I guess, inoffensive. Was Nigel in the choir? Pretty certain he wasn't.

Not that I thought that at the time of course. What I do remember is feeling affected, being let down somehow. Like Miss McKay had snubbed me, somehow. In every other sense it was something that came and went. It was just one of those things that occasionally niggled. And the probationer badge - the one that was blue, not the main event, which was red - was somehow cold comfort.

No, it looks like this was the first political decision intended to oust me - the first of many, haha. And it was no coincidence that its effect came just before it was time to go.

So... back to the St. Thomas' Entrance Exam. Did I say Matchbox multi-storey carpark? Well, actually, that was for Nigel taking the exam. I got nothing for taking my exam. Why should I?

Nigel's parents were genuinely groovy but they had no problem doting on their darling boy. And maybe there was something else. Maybe they thought he didn't quite have what it took to step up to the plate - to do his own thing. Maybe they just accepted the fact that Nigel Benton was just destined to be a Benton's Beds boy all his life. That he would need any incentive going to do anything outside of his comfort zone. Like taking an exam. Because if he didn't get what he wanted, then maybe he just wouldn't do that uncomfortable thing, however objectively mild.

Maybe this was all part of something else, something more unsavoury. Maybe they felt they couldn't control him at all. Because Nigel was essentially a Bad Boy. A boy who just had to be left, had to be mollified. Maybe he cried too much as a baby. Maybe he threw all his toys out of the cot. My experience of him, more often than I care to remember, is that he could be too much of a boy. Like the time when I visited the Posh House with the Posh Pool and we gathered conkers together. With his friend Tim.

"They're too small. They're pathetic. Tim, pick them up."

So, Tim picked them up and threw them at me, one by one, tauntingly. Not that I could be taunted. I wasn't that kind of boy. Because I wasn't a Boy at all, of course. All I could do is take the chucking, take the taunting, take the rejection. As they walked off and I was left, just outside the front of the house, to my own devices, I remembered that crushing feeling of isolation, not realising that walking away, for good, was the only solution. I could have walked back into the house, rung home (I was old enough to remember our number and use the phone, after all) and that would have been that. But because, for some reason, I felt that staying in the Nigel fold was advantageous somehow, that rejecting him would increase the Threat, I just said nothing, sat in their front room and waited.

More fool me.

That Entrance Exam. Miss Higgins told me about it. "You have an exam for St. Thomas's coming up. And we're going to teach you how to pass it. There'll be extra lessons after school and at lunchtimes. For the next term. Then you'll take the entrance exam. Take these books. We'll start on Monday". Part of her extraordinary teaching skill. To be straight and never waver.

And the boys school. Well it was strange, different. And the procedure was really quite straightforward. I didn't just pass it, apparently. Not that I knew that. This highfaluting, austere place seemed so beyond me, so out of sight. I remember that when I got called for the interview, how surprised I was that I managed to get to that stage. Then I remember how kind the Headmaster seemed to be, which surprised me too as I was expecting someone quite unreachable. He asked me quite good, quite interesting questions, questions which seemed to take an interest in me, like what I was interested in and what I wanted to be - that kind of thing.

Mum was never one for hiding things from me, particularly when it came to anything related to my own achievements as she found it difficult to shield her glow. When I learned I got in I was very happy and excited. Then when she told me that I'd come top of all candidates I couldn't actually believe it. I still can't. I imagine she made it up. That maybe I came in the top 10 or something and assume that she'd exaggerated or deliberately hid the truth form herself.

I've always had an issue with attainment. I've craved it then on the occasions when it's happened I've almost disbelieved it. So that might explain why I never consider myself to have achieved anything. Except perhaps from being a father.

Nigel, however, attained to gain.

I loved his toys, I'll admit it. I was vicarious. I lived his super-duper Matchbox multi-storey. And what an edifice it truly was. A majestic structure, 2 feet from the ground, with a fully-working petrol station at its base, authentic lane dividers and parking bays. At the time I don't think I'd even seen a real one before, let alone a toy one. I was in awe of this thing and treated it with the deference it deserved.

But that wasn't all. Nigel duly passed the exam too (though of course he wasn't placed) and for that achievement he got the Matchbox transporter. An altogether more advanced piece of engineering than the car park. A bridge, a car-cage and a pulley mechanism - this was most definitely for the boy who had more than everything. The King of Boys who had devoured so many toys he required the ultimate pleasure experience - the challenge of transporting a small metal object with wheels across an imaginary ravine.

Of course, I never got the hang of it.

And Nigel? Well, his parents' approach paid off. He became MD of Benton's Beds. And remained so for the rest of his working days.

Just after my interview, after Mum and I had spoken with the kind Headmaster and he'd told me I was "in", we went to the fabulous toy shop on Broad Street, just 100 yards from the school and she bought me a black & white plastic football. The kind that floats in the wind, that isn't straight and true. My prize.

I think I'd deserved it

CHAPTER 25

Extraordinary: Summer Trips
and Summer Fêtes

Two things that made a 7 year-old in Spring and Summer 1972 almost freeze with excitement.

Can you remember when you went on your first ever school trip? Or outing? Isn't that a great word? It's the sort of feeling you forget, isn't it? But put yourself in a quiet corner for a moment. Shut your eyes. If I say, "Did Mum pack your sandwiches?", what do you feel?

Indeed.

Particularly if you'd been used to school dinners all that time. Which most of us back then had been.

It actually felt special. To be given a packed lunch. With egg and cucumber sandwiches. A packet of Smiths Crisps. Salt and vinegar. Or cheese and onion. Or both! Can of Coke!

Thought "special" isn't quite right. Free? Exciting? I don't know, English is so useless sometimes. Breathless? Close. Shimmering, perhaps. Or just a combination.

The packed lunch was a symbol. It symbolised the unusual, the unlikely, the different. It didn't matter how much or little I enjoyed or accepted the day - as you know, I accepted the day pretty well - *that* felt good. Wondrous.

And next. I remember not going into school. Wow! I think we met outside and clambered straight onto the coach. Of course, it wasn't just me who was on the cusp of wetting myself. It was the other girls too. Even Nigel!

Of course there was a time when I saw occasional TV footage of kids jumping up and down or, worse, friends' video posts with their insipid and asinine comments about how brave, pretty, inspiring, intelligent their darlings were, that my spirits plunged.

Recently, though, I've remembered. Just how I reacted to my own special occasions. How I felt and how that feels now. And how important that feeling is.

How dead are we to feelings these days?

We'd chatter, Nigel and me, all the way to Brokerswood. And there'd be Victoria, straining and peering between the head-rests. Or Judy and Catherine, next to us, passing us an Opal Fruit each.

Chatter. Anything. From what was on page 3 of Jane's I-Spy book to why Morecambe was funnier than Dick Emery or why Nigel actually liked Tich and Quackers. Nigel brought his yellow tonka toy. I said, "You're not allowed". I was promptly put right by Miss HIggins. Must have been a little jealous.

The journey seemed to last an age. Actually it took 45 minutes.

Then out.

We must have been to Brokerswood at least three times while I was at The School. It was a large (well, we thought it was large, anyway) expanse of Wiltshire wilderness (well, we thought it was wilderness) nestled in the Savernake forest in Wiltshire. If I'm entirely honest, I remember feeling a little underwhelmed the first time we went. Must have been expecting the journey to last longer, my disappointment rooted in the fiction that the further you went from home the more exotic things would become.

Once I'd become used to the proximity issue I absolutely loved it. It was beautiful. It smelled like Brokerswood was supposed to smell like too. Dankly atmospheric Of course it nearly always rained. And Mrs Thompson (we were sharing teachers that day) would try to identify things - birds mostly.

"That's a chaffinch. No, woodpecker. Hold on, it's a black-bird".

"Cuckoo, Miss."

"What?"

"Cuckoo. My Dad takes me birdwatching, Miss".

"Everyone knows that's a cuckoo, Judy."

"Stop it, Nigel."

We'd traipse for what seemed like all day.

Then we'd settle down with our packed lunch. Or, in my case, half a sandwich. I just hadn't been able to resist.

And then. The most important, most pant-wetting part of our outing.

The shop.

Just to look was enough. Exotic woodland treats. Pens with half-printed squirrels. More I-Spy books than you could shake a twig at. Walking sticks. And gobstoppers.

Can't remember why they were there.

To this day, I'm never quite sure why my pocket money didn't extend to school outings. I think I'd been given 20p as a special treat. That was about enough to buy a pencil and another can of Coke.

Nigel, naturally enough, bought the whole shop.

For me, though, it was enough just to stand in that shop. The perfect end to another memorable trip.

And although no one ever said much on the way back, you could always rely on Judy.

"Blue Tit, Miss."

*****

And the other special event? The grand school finale?

What else!

It was the middle of July. Through the back entrance, stepping down through the cracked paving, through the greens and browns, yellows, blues and greys, I looked ahead. Deep blue sky, cotton wool clouds. For the first time this summer, covering the city. Ahead to the tennis courts, slightly left to the funny grey block, then round and left again to the entrance to the old school.

I seemed to have grown up.

Of course, it would never have been called School Fair. This was Bankton High, the school for nice young ladies.

The School Fête was a kaleidoscopic, colourful cornucopia of everything a middle class community could throw back at its daughters' growth establishment.

Victoria sponge, cherry cake, shortbread, coffee cake, Battenberg, Bath Buns. One table.

Battling Tops, Scrabble, Lego sets, Meccano kits from 1953, Kerplunk, Stickle bricks, Monopoly, Ludo board with frayed edges and Tiddlywinks. Another.

Old comics, books and annuals. Famous Five. Wiliam. Beano, Twinkle, Topper, Cor, Vantage, Bunty, Sparky, Beezer. Bleep & Booster, Magpie. Look-In. Boys and girls stuff.

Dolls. Barbie, Sasha, Sindy, Action Man, Tiny Tears, Whimsies, Trolls, Gonks.

Baking kits, empty milk trucks and dolls houses,

And there were more. What seemed like hundreds more.

Bracelets and necklaces (mostly pearl) for Mum, old capacitors for Dad. Even a rusty woman's bicycle.

Flipping brilliant.

Something cooked up or thrown out, for the whole family.

Tombola. And this year the special prize, just like last year and the year before that... a black and white portable telly! Who would win that? Had to be someone special. Couldn't be one of us, surely.

This fête was of course particularly special to both Nigel and me. It was the very last time we would be officially be Bankton High School Girls. The end of something, so to speak. We weren't quite sure what but it was definitely the end.

And we were going out in style. By getting lost. With some other girls.

Think it was Zarah, Jane, Catherine (Judy was already on holiday), Debbie, NIgel and me. We'd taken time away from our parents ("see you later!" "ah, that's lovely"), walked onto the grassy slope just past the rockery by the back entrances, past the pine trees at the top, just above us and just kept walking straight on, into the fields where those maidens with urns, the ones in the Gold books, must have been, hundreds and hundreds of years ago.

"Let's play Pig!". Pig was tag and Pig was chaser. Pig had to touch the chased and oink at the same time. Then chased became Pig.

I was first Zarah was lithe and quick and never got caught. Usually it was Debbie, who was a little slower than the rest of us but this time I got lucky with Nigel and caught him just as he was about to dive into a thick clump of long grass near the wall at the top.

"Oink".

"You weren't loud enough!"

"Was!"

"Weren't"

"Your turn, Nigel!" Victoria? Well now, who'd have thought!

That Summer feeling.

Nigel had to turn and race down the hill. His face was getting uncommonly red with rage. Peter had found his feet though and was heading straight for the willow with the uncommonly thick trunk smack in the middle of the field. By the time Nigel had caught up I managed to dart swiftly behind the tree just as Nigel had raised his arm. Next thing I heard was a rasping crack.

Then a very loud wail.

I really can't remember how six seven-year olds managed to cope with the pain and drama without their parents on hand but we must have done pretty well as, not fifteen minutes later, we were back in their midst, tales having been told (not all of which were completely true) and Nigel whisked off to the Royal United, which made his summer as it turned out, as there's nothing a boy with more than everything likes more than to be spoiled inordinately, the eager recipient of signatures, self-portraits and T-Rex logos, all revealing very little of that once smooth and brilliantly white plaster cast.

And us girls? Well, we spent the rest of that sublime Saturday giggling uncontrollably and rolling down that grass bank under those trees at the back of that now decommissioned and demolished girls public day school on the north side of the utterly beautiful but tarnished city of Bath in the West of England.

CHAPTER 26

Who's really to blame?

Recently I've been thinking, "Am I making too much of all this? Because, essentially, I don't think I ever got to know any these girls. Not properly".

I remember their names. I remember what they looked like - even what they felt like. But did I ever get to spend much time with any? Did I ever, in fact, have the kind of relationship most of them had with each other?

Of course not. Because, as much as I became a girl, I was still a boy. And it made much more sense, to them and their mothers at any rate. Girls should gravitate towards girls. Boys should know their place.

Or maybe they didn't even consider it. Maybe the girls just decided on their own kind in a more feral way.

Or maybe I'm completely wrong about all that too.

It's just that I never remember, Fenella excepted - we were thrust upon each other in any case - coming home with Judy, Catherine, Jane, Zarah, Judy, Debbie or any other girl from that class for that matter in tow. Oh, don't be silly, Peter, you were 6 not 16.

It still weighs on my mind. Wny? It happened such a long time ago. But, you see, time is always frozen. So long as you remember it, or even think you do, it's there, in the present, reminding you of who you actually are, who you're supposed to be.

Because, today and for as long as I can remember, I know my way with women, with men too. I'm the steady one, the safe pair of hands, wise old Peter. The Inscrutable One. Probably.

There's mutual admiration, affection, respect. But it all seems distant, so temporal. Temporary.

And the link is rarely there. The link where you just gravitate, naturally. To your own.

Do I ask too much? Is that Mum's fault? Did she shower me with too much in those days? Boost the ego to 11? Keep my expectations high of myself and of others? Only to see them eroded as I approached adulthood and beyond?

No one sees this of course. That's the problem perhaps. For those who are more than happy (if that's the right word) their trials, tribulations and deepest pain there seems to be a special prize - that of an instant gang of cheerleaders, driving them on, powering them towards a new life of optimism, vigour and a new form of prosperity. Peter never got that. Maybe because he wasn't prepared to show his low-esteem in that way. Or maybe because he didn't trust the world enough.

Blame is a dreadful thing. It leads to very little. When you look to your past for answers to the loneliness, the lack of achievement or contentment or joy, there's a kind of dopamine fix where you might say, "That's it, that's the reason why I'm like I am. That's good. I've found it. Now I can explain it and it feels better". Like being sent to a girl's school between 4 and 7. "That was odd. That was great. But it was wrong. "

You attach the blame to that thing and there's your answer. Then you can explain it to the world.

The world won't listen to that, though. They're far more interested in how that odd situation makes them feel about themselves. In every detail possible.

And there's the thing, Peter. Right there. If you're really looking for answers - a route to happiness, it doesn't stop with blame. In fact, you should bypass blame altogether. And you don't have to share your pain, certainly not the present pain of age, remorse or dissatisfaction with your lot.

What you can share is your story.

Shouldn't we all?

EPILOGUE

The story of a little girl who goes to a boys school

First day of new school. Nervous but not so nervous as to think that I was wasn't "The Chosen One", the one who'd made The Grade. Got top marks. Been a Good Boy.

I should have taken more notice of my adrenalin.

First hour was memorable - it was different. I was seated next to a slightly awkward boy called Timothy. Of course he was called Timothy. Didn't feel the same as meeting a girl for the first time. Slightly empty. So I can only remember his awkwardness, nothing much more.

The only other person in that first hour I can remember was a boy called Tom. Toogood. Of course he was called Toogood. It was as if the teachers had pinned a skull and crossbones sign on his head.

There was one more thing in that first hour. Surnames. It was clear that from now on our first names would be deleted and I would be known simply as "True".

After that hour.

A playground. 80 by 40 feet. 3 high walls. With the school back wall completing the square. And 350 boys. Hard plastic spheres. A selection process. What was this? Boys' introduction to a boy's life? Of course. And I was Last One.

On the first day.

A small boy. Who'd been a girl. 7 years, 9 months and 20 days. Standing against a high, grey wall. Footballs flying at high velocity. Head height. The very worst 15 minutes of a small life thus far.

Like I said, my parents meant well.

Printed in Great Britain
by Amazon